KT-119-890

Crouching down in front of the grate, he watched as she began to blow on the flames to coax them into life, and Tariq found his eyes drawn to the skirt—which had now stretched tightly over her curves.

He swallowed down a sudden, debilitating leap of desire, which made him harden in a way he wasn't expecting. In five years of close contact with his highly efficient assistant, he could never remember noticing her bottom before. And it was actually a rather fine bottom. Firm and high and beautifully rounded. The kind of bottom a man liked to cup in the palms of his hands as he was…

'What?' Isobel turned round and frowned.

'I didn't…' Tariq swallowed.

What the hell was going on? Did bumps to the head make men lose their senses, so that they started imagining all kinds of inappropriate things?

'I didn't say anything.'

'But you made a funny sort of noise.' Her eyes narrowed as she looked at him. 'Are you all right? Your eyes have gone all glazed.'

'Are you surprised?' Shifting his position, Tariq glared at her, willing his arousal to subside. 'I've just had to endure your driving.'

Sharon Kendrick started story-telling at the age of eleven, and has never really stopped. She likes to write fast-paced, feel-good romances, with heroes who are so sexy they'll make your toes curl!

Born in west London, she now lives in the beautiful city of Winchester—where she can see the cathedral from her window (but only if she stands on tiptoe). She has two children, Celia and Patrick, and her passions include music, books, cooking and eating—and drifting off into wonderful daydreams while she works out new plots!

Recent titles by the same author:

MONARCH OF THE SANDS
THE FORBIDDEN INNOCENT
TOO PROUD TO BE BOUGHT

Did you know these are also available as eBooks?
Visit www.millsandboon.co.uk

THE SHEIKH'S UNDOING

BY
SHARON KENDRICK

All the characters in this book have no existence outside the imagination of the author, and have no relation whatsoever to anyone bearing the same name or names. They are not even distantly inspired by any individual known or unknown to the author, and all the incidents are pure invention.

All Rights Reserved including the right of reproduction in whole or in part in any form. This edition is published by arrangement with Harlequin Enterprises II BV/S.à.r.l. The text of this publication or any part thereof may not be reproduced or transmitted in any form or by any means, electronic or mechanical, including photocopying, recording, storage in an information retrieval system, or otherwise, without the written permission of the publisher.

® and TM are trademarks owned and used by the trademark owner and/or its licensee. Trademarks marked with ® are registered with the United Kingdom Patent Office and/or the Office for Harmonisation in the Internal Market and in other countries.

First published in Great Britain 2012
by Mills & Boon, an imprint of Harlequin (UK) Limited.
Harlequin (UK) Limited, Eton House, 18-24 Paradise Road,
Richmond, Surrey TW9 1SR

© Sharon Kendrick 2012

ISBN: 978 0 263 22640 9

Harlequin (UK) policy is to use papers that are natural, renewable and recyclable products and made from wood grown in sustainable forests. The logging and manufacturing process conform to the legal environmental regulations of the country of origin.

Printed and bound in Great Britain
by CPI Antony Rowe, Chippenham, Wiltshire

THE SHEIKH'S UNDOING

MORAY COUNCIL LIBRARIES & INFO.SERVICES	
20 33 82 90	
Askews & Holts	
RF	

CHAPTER ONE

THE sound of the telephone woke her, but Isobel didn't need to see the name flashing on the screen to know who was ringing. Who else would call her at this time of night but the man who thought he had the right to do pretty much whatever he wanted? And frequently did.

Tariq, the so-called 'Playboy Prince'. Or Prince Tariq Kadar al Hakam, Sheikh of Khayarzah—to give him his full and rather impressive title. And the boss if not exactly from hell then certainly from some equally dark and complicated place.

She glanced at the clock. Four in the morning was early even by *his* standards. Yawning, she picked up the phone, wondering what the hell he had been up to this time.

Had some new story about him emerged, as it so often did, sparked by gossip about his latest audacious take-over bid? Or had he simply got himself tied up with a new blonde—they were always blonde—and wanted Isobel to juggle his early morning meetings for him? Would he walk into the office later on with yesterday's growth darkening his strong jaw and a smug smile curving the edges of his sensual lips? And the scent of someone's perfume still lingering on his skin...

It wouldn't be the first time it had happened, that was for sure. With a frown, Isobel recalled some of his more famous sexual conquests, before reminding herself that she was employed as his personal assistant—not his moral guardian.

Friends sometimes asked whether she ever tired of having a boss who demanded so much of her. Or whether she was tempted to tell him exactly what she thought of his outrageously chauvinistic behaviour—and the answer was yes. Sometimes. But the generous amount of money he paid her soon put a stop to her disapproval. Because money like that provided security—the kind of security which you could never get from another person. Isobel knew that better than anyone. Hadn't her mother taught her that the most important lesson a woman could learn was to be completely independent of men? Men could just walk away whenever they wanted...and because they could, they frequently did.

She answered the call. 'Hello?'

'I-Isobel?'

Her senses were instantly alerted when she heard the deep voice of her employer—because there was something very different about it. Either he was in some kind of post-coital daze or something was wrong. Because he sounded...*weird.*

She'd never heard Tariq hesitate before. Never heard him as anything other than the confident and charismatic Prince—the darling of London's casinos and international gossip columns. The man most women couldn't resist, even when—as seemed inevitable—he was destined to break their heart into tiny little pieces.

'Tariq?' Isobel's voice took on a sudden note of urgency. 'Is something wrong?'

From amid a painful throbbing, which felt as if a thousand hammers were beating against his skull, Tariq registered the familiar voice of his assistant. His first brush with reality after what seemed like hours of chaos and confusion. Almost imperceptibly he let out a low sigh of relief as his lashes parted by a fraction. Izzy was his anchor. Izzy would sort this out for him. A ceiling swam into view, and quickly he shut his eyes against its harsh brightness.

'Accident,' he mumbled.

'Accident?' Isobel sat up in bed, her heart thundering as she heard the unmistakable twist of pain in his voice. 'What kind of accident? Tariq, where are you? What's *happened?*'

'I…'

'Tariq?' Isobel could hear someone indignantly telling him that he shouldn't be using his phone, and then a rustling noise before a woman's voice came on the line.

'Hello?' the strange voice said. 'Who is this, please?'

Isobel felt fear begin to whisper over her as she recognised the sound of officialdom, and it took an almighty effort just to stop her voice from shaking. 'M-my name is Isobel Mulholland and I work for Sheikh al Hakam— would you please tell me what's going on?'

There was a pause before the woman spoke again. 'This is one of the staff nurses at the Accident and Emergency department of St Mark's hospital in Chislehurst. I'm afraid that the Sheikh has been involved in a car crash—'

'Is he okay?' Isobel interrupted.

'I'm afraid I can't give out any more information at the moment.'

Hearing inflexible resistance in the woman's voice,

Isobel swung her legs over the side of the bed. 'I'm on my way,' she said grimly, and cut the connection.

Pulling on a pair of jeans, she grabbed the first warm sweater which came to hand and then, after shoving her still-bare feet into sheepskin boots, took the elevator down to the underground car park of her small London apartment.

Thank heavens for sat-nav, she thought as she tapped in the name of the hospital and waited for a map to appear on the screen. She peered at it. It seemed that Chislehurst was on the edge of the Kent countryside—less than an hour from here, especially at this time in the morning.

But, even though there was barely any traffic around, Isobel had to force herself to concentrate on the road ahead and not focus on the frightened thoughts which were crowding into her mind.

What the hell was Tariq doing driving around at this time in the morning? And what was he doing *crashing his car*—he who was normally as adept at driving as he was at riding one of his polo ponies?

Her fingers tightened around the steering wheel as she tried and failed to imagine her powerful boss lying injured. But it was an image which stubbornly failed to materialise, for he was a man who was larger than life in every sense of the word.

Tall and striking, with distinctive golden-dark colouring, Sheikh Tariq al Hakam commanded attention wherever he was. Complete strangers stopped to watch him walk by in the street. Women pressed their phone numbers into his hand in restaurants. She'd seen it happen time and time again. His proud and sometimes cruel features had often been compared to those of a fallen angel. And he exuded such passion and energy that it was impossible to imagine anything inhibiting those qualities—even for a second.

What if...? Isobel swallowed down the acrid taste of fear. What if her charismatic boss was in *danger?* What would she do if he was in a life-threatening condition? If he...he...

She'd never thought of Tariq as mortal before, and now she could think of nothing else. Her heart missed a beat as she registered the blaring horn of a passing car and she tightened her fingers on the steering wheel. There was no point in thinking negatively. Whatever it was, he would pull through—just like he always did. Because Tariq was as strong as a lion, and she couldn't imagine anything dimming that magnificent strength of his.

A dull rain was spattering against the windscreen as she pulled into the hospital car park. It was still so early that the morning staff hadn't yet arrived. The whole building seemed eerily quiet as she entered it, which only increased her growing sense of foreboding. Noiselessly, she sped down the bright corridors towards the A&E department until she reached the main desk.

A nurse glanced up at her. 'Can I help you?'

Isobel wiped a raindrop from her cheek. 'I've come... I'm here about one of your patients. His name is Tariq al Hakam and I understand he's been involved in a car crash.'

'And you are?' enquired the nurse, her carefully plucked eyebrows disappearing beneath her fringe.

'I work for him.'

'I'm afraid I can't tell you anything,' said the nurse,

with a dismissive smile. 'You aren't his next of kin, are you?'

Isobel shook her head. 'His next of kin lives in the Middle East,' she said. Swallowing down her frustration, she realised that she'd crammed her thick curls into a ponytail and thrown on a pair of old jeans and a sweater. Did she look unbelievably scruffy? The last kind of person who would be associated with the powerful Sheikh? Was that the reason the nurse was being so...so...*officious?* 'I work closely with the Prince and have done for the past five years,' she continued urgently. 'Please let me see him. I'm...I'm...'

For one stupid moment she was about to say *I'm all he's got.* Until she realised that the shock of hearing he was injured must have temporarily unhinged her mind. Why, Tariq had a whole *stable* of women he could call upon in an instant. Women who were far closer to him than Isobel had ever been or ever would be.

'I'm the person he rang just over an hour ago,' she said, her voice full of appeal. 'It was...it was me he turned to.'

The nurse looked at her steadily, and then seemed to take pity on her.

'He has a concussion,' she said quietly, and then shook her head as if in answer to the silent question in Isobel's eyes. 'His CT scan shows no sign of haemorrhaging, but we're putting him under observation just to be sure.'

No sign of haemorrhaging. A breath of relief shuddered from Isobel's lips, and for a moment she had to lean on the nurses' station for support. 'Thank you,' she whispered. 'Can I *see* him? Please? Would that be okay? Just for a moment.'

There was a moment's assessment, and then the nurse nodded. 'Well, as long as it *is* a moment. A familiar face is often reassuring. But you're not to excite him—do you understand?'

Isobel gave a wry smile. 'Oh, there's no danger of that happening,' she answered—because Tariq thought she was about as exciting as watching paint dry.

He'd often described her as the most practical and sensible woman he knew—citing those as the reasons he employed her. Once, she'd even overheard him saying that it was a relief to find a woman under thirty who wasn't a *distraction,* and although it had hurt at the time, she could live with it. She'd always known her place in his life and that wasn't about to change now. Her job was to soothe his ruffled feathers, not to excite him. There were plenty of other contenders for *that* category.

She followed the rhythmical squishing of the nurse's rubber-soled shoes into a side-room at the far end of the unit, and the unbelievable sight that confronted her there made her heart skip a painful beat.

Shrouded in the bleached cotton of a single sheet lay the prone figure of her boss. He looked too long and too broad for the narrow hospital bed, and he was lying perfectly still. The stark white bedlinen threw his darkly golden colouring into relief—and even from here she could see the dark red stain of blood which had matted his thick black hair.

Waves of dizziness washed over her at the sight of the seemingly indestructible Tariq looking so stricken, and Isobel had to quash a stupid instinct to run over to his side and touch her fingers to his cheek. But the nurse had warned her not to excite him, and so she mustered up her usual level-headed attitude and walked quietly towards him.

His eyes were closed—two ebony feathered arcs of lashes were lying against a face which she could see was unusually blanched, despite the natural darkness of his olive skin.

She swallowed down the acid taste of fear. She had seen Tariq in many different guises during the five eventful years she'd been working for him. She'd seen him looking sharp and urbanely suited as he dominated the boardroom during the meetings which filled his life. She'd seen him hollow-eyed from lack of sleep when he'd spent most of the night gambling and had come straight into the office brandishing a thick wad of notes and a careless smile.

Once she'd started remembering Isobel couldn't stop. Other images crowded into her mind. Tariq in jodhpurs as he played polo with such breathtaking flair, and the faint sheen of sweat that made his muddy jodhpurs stick to his powerful thighs. Tariq in jeans and a T-shirt when he was dressed down and casual. Or looking like a movie idol in a sharply tailored tuxedo before he went out to dinner. She'd even seen him in the flowing white robes and headdress of his homeland, when he was leaving on one of his rare visits to the oil-rich kingdom of Khayarzah—where his brother Zahid was King.

But she had never seen her powerful boss looking so defenceless before, and something inside her softened and melted. At that moment she felt almost *tender* towards him—as if she'd like to cradle him in her arms and comfort him. Poor, vulnerable Tariq she thought bleakly.

Until the reality of the situation came slamming

home to her and she forced herself to confront it. Tariq was looking vulnerable because right at this moment he *was.* Very vulnerable. Lying injured on a hospital bed. Beneath the wool of her sweater she could feel the crash of her heart—and she had to fight back a feeling of panic, and nausea.

'Tariq,' she breathed softly. 'Oh, Tariq.'

Tariq screwed up his eyes. Through the mists of hammering pain he was aware of something familiar and yet curiously different about the woman who was speaking to him. It was a voice he knew well. A voice which exemplified the small area of calm which lay at the centre of his crazy life. It was... *Izzy's* voice, he realised—but not as he'd ever heard it before. Normally it was crisp and matter-of-fact, sometimes cool and disapproving, but he'd never heard it all soft and trembling before.

His eyes opened, surprising a look of such darkened fear in her gaze that he was momentarily taken aback. He studied the soft quiver of her lips and felt the tiptoeing of something unfamiliar on his skin. Was that really Izzy?

'Don't worry. I'm not about to die,' he drawled. And then, despite the terrible aching at his temples, he allowed just the right pause for maximum effect before directing a mocking question at the woman in uniform who was standing beside his bed, her fingertips counting the hammering of his pulse. 'Am I, Nurse?'

Inexplicably, Isobel felt angry at Tariq for being as arrogant as only he knew how. He could have killed himself, and all he could do was flirt with the damned nurse! Why had she wasted even a second being sentimental about him when she should have realised that he was as indestructible as a rock? And with about as much emotion as a rock, too! She wanted to tell him not to dare be so flippant—but, recognising that might fall into the category of exciting him, she bit back the words.

'What happened?' she questioned, still having to fight the stupid desire to touch him.

Bunching her wistful fingers into a tight fist by her side, she stared down at the hawkish lines of his auto-cratic face.

'You may not be the slowest driver in the world, but you're usually careful,' she said. And then seeing the nurse glare at her, Isobel remembered that she was sup-posed to be calming him, not quizzing him. 'No, don't bother answering that,' she added hastily. 'In fact, don't even think about it. Just lie there—and rest.'

Black brows were elevated in disbelief. 'You aren't usually quite so agreeable,' he observed caustically.

'Well, these aren't usual circumstances, are they?'

Isobel gave what she hoped was a reassuring smile—but it wasn't easy to keep the panic at bay. Not when all she wanted to do was take him in her arms and tell him that everything was going to be all right. To rest his cheek against the mad racing of her heart and lace her fingers through the inky silk of his hair and stroke it. What on earth was the *matter* with her?

'You've just got to lie there quietly and let the nurses take care of you and check that you're in one p-piece.'

That unfamiliar tremble in her voice was back, and Tariq's eyes narrowed as her face swam in and out of focus. Funny. He couldn't really remember looking at Izzy's face before. Or maybe he had—just not like this. In the normal progression of a day you never really stared at a woman for a long time. Not unless you were planning to seduce her.

But for once there was nowhere else to look. He could see the freckles standing out like sentries against her pale skin, and her amber eyes looked as if they would be more at home on a startled kitten. She looked *soft,* he thought suddenly. *Cute.* As if she might curl into the crook of his arm and lie there purring all afternoon.

Shaking his head in order to rid himself of this temporary hallucination, he glared at her.

'It'll take more than a car crash or a nurse to make me lie quietly,' he said, impatiently moving one leg—which had started to itch like no itch he could remember. As he bent his knee, the sheet concertinaed down to his groin and one hair-roughened thigh was revealed. And despite the pain and the bizarre circumstances he could not resist the flicker of a smile as both the nurse and Isobel gave an involuntary little gasp before quickly averting their eyes.

'Lets just cover you up, shall we?' questioned the nurse briskly, her cheeks growing bright pink as she tugged the sheet back in place.

Isobel felt similarly hot and bothered as she realised that her handsome boss was completely naked beneath the sheet. That, unless she was very much mistaken, the sheet seemed to be moving of its own accord around his groin area. She wasn't the most experienced cookie in the tin but even she knew what *that* meant. It was a shockingly intimate experience, which started a heated prickling of her skin in response. And that was a first.

Because—unlike just about every other female with a pulse—she was immune to Tariq al Hakim and his sex appeal. His hard, muscular body left her completely cold—as did those hawk-like features and the ebony glitter of his dark-lashed eyes. She didn't go for men

who were self-professed playboys—sexy, dangerous
men who knew exactly the kind of effect they had on
women. Who could walk away from the women who
loved them without a backward glance. In fact, those
were precisely the men she tended to despise. The ones
her mother had warned her against. Men like her own
father—who could shrug off emotion and responsibility so easily…

Composing herself with a huge effort of will, she
turned to the nurse. 'What happens now?' she asked
but Tariq answered before the woman in uniform had a
chance to.

'I get off this damned bed and you drive me to the office. That's what happens,' he snapped. But as he tried
to sit up the stupid shooting pain made him slump back
against the bed again, and he groaned and then glared
at her again as if it was all *her* fault.

'Will you please *lie still,* Prince al Hakam?' ordered
the nurse crisply, before turning to Isobel. 'The doctors
would like to keep the Sheikh in for twenty-four hours'
observation.'

'Izzy,' said Tariq, and as Isobel turned to him his
black eyes glinted with the kind of steely determination
she recognised so well. 'Sort this out for me, will you?
There's no way I'm staying in this damned hospital for
a minute longer.'

For a moment Isobel didn't speak. There were many
times when she admired her boss—because nobody
could deny his drive, his determination, his unerr-
ing nose for success. But his arrogance and sheer self-
belief sometimes had the potential to be his downfall.
Like now.

'Look, this isn't some business deal you're masterminding,' she said crossly. 'This is your *health* we're talking about—and you're not the expert here, Tariq, the doctors and nurses are. They don't want to keep you in because it's some sort of *fun*—I can't imagine it's much fun having *you* as a patient—but because it's necessary. And if you don't start listening to them and doing what they say, then I'm going to walk out of here right now and leave you to get on with it.'

There was a pause as Tariq's eyes narrowed angrily. 'But I have meetings—'

'I know precisely what meetings you have,' she interrupted, her voice gentling suddenly as she registered the strain which was etched on his face. 'I organise your diary, don't I? I'll sort everything out back at the office and you're not to worry about a thing. Do you…?' She found herself staring down at the white hospital sheet which now seemed to be stretched uncomfortably tight across the muscular expanse of his torso. 'Do you want me to get hold of some pyjamas for you?'

'Pyjamas?' His mouth curved into a smile which mocked her almost as much as the lazy glitter of his eyes. 'You think I'm the kind of man who wears pyjamas, do you, Izzy?'

Inexplicably, her heart began to pound with unwilling excitement—and Isobel was furious at her reaction. Had he seen it—and was that why his smile had now widened into an arrogant smirk? 'Your choice of nightwear isn't something I've given a lot of thought to,' she answered crossly. 'But I'll take that as a no. Is there anything else you want?'

Tariq winced as he recalled the blood-stained and crumpled clothing which was stuffed into a plastic bag in the locker next to his bed. 'Just bring me some clean clothes, can you? And a razor?'

'Of course. And as soon as the doctors give you the thumbs-up I'll come and get you. Is that okay?'

There was a pause as their gazes met. 'You don't really want me to answer that, do you?' he questioned, closing his eyes as a sudden and powerful fatigue washed over him. It was like no feeling he'd ever experienced and it left him feeling debilitated. Weak. The last thing he wanted was for his assistant to see him looking weak. 'Just go, will you, Izzy?' he added wearily.

Slipping silently from the room, Isobel walked until she stepped out into the brightening light of the spring morning. Sucking in a deep breath, she felt a powerful sense of relief washing over her. Tariq was alive. That was the main thing. He might have had a nasty knock to the head, but hopefully he hadn't done any lasting damage. And yet... She bit her lip as she climbed into her car and started up the engine, her thoughts still in turmoil. How *alone* he had looked on that narrow hospital bed.

The loud tooting of a car made her glance into the driving mirror, where she caught a glimpse of her pale and unwashed face. A touch of reality began to return.

Alone?

Tariq?

Why, there were innumerable women who would queue around the block to put paid to that particular myth with no more incentive than the elevation of one black and arrogant eyebrow and that mocking smile. Tariq had plenty of people to take care of him, she reminded herself. He didn't need *her.*

Arriving back in London, she spent the rest of the day cancelling meetings and dealing with the calls which flooded in from his associates. She worked steadily until eight, then went over to his apartment—a vast penthouse in a tall building which overlooked Green Park. Although she held a spare set of keys, she'd only ever been there once before, when she had delivered a package which the Sheikh had been expecting and which had arrived very late at the office, while she'd still been working. Rather than having it couriered round to him, Isobel had decided to take it there herself.

It had been one of the most embarrassing occasions of her life, because a tousle-headed Tariq had answered the door wearing what was clearly a hastily pulled on silk dressing gown. His face had been faintly flushed as he'd taken the package from her, and she hadn't needed to hear the breathless female voice calling his name to realise that he had company.

But it had been his almost *helpless* shrug which had infuriated her more than anything. The way his black eyes had met hers and he'd bestowed on her one of his careless smiles. As if he was inviting her to join him in a silent conspiracy of wondering why he was just so irresistible to women. She remembered thrusting the package into his hands and stomping off home to an empty apartment, cursing the arrogance of the Playboy Prince.

Closing her mind to the disturbing memory, Isobel let herself into the apartment using the complicated trio of keys. Experience made her listen for a moment. But everything was silent—which meant that his servants had all gone home for the evening.

In his dressing room she found jeans, cashmere sweaters and a leather jacket—and added a warm scarf. But when it came to selecting some boxer shorts from the silken pile which were heaped neatly in a drawer, she found herself blushing for the second time that day. How...*intimate* it was to be rifling through Tariq's underwear. Underwear which had clung to the oiled silk of his olive skin...

Frustrated with the wayward trajectory of her thoughts, she threw the clothes into an overnight bag and let herself out. Then she phoned the hospital, to be told that the Sheikh's condition was satisfactory and that if he continued to improve then he could be discharged the next day.

But the press had got wind of his crash—despite the reassuring statement which Isobel had asked his PR people to issue. Fabulously wealthy injured sheikhs always provided fascinating copy, and by the time she arrived back at the hospital the following morning there were photographers hanging around the main entrance.

Tariq had been transferred to a different side ward, and Isobel walked in to see a small gaggle of doctors gathered around the foot of his bed. There was an unmistakable air of tension in the room.

She shot a glance at her boss, who was sitting up in bed, unshaven and unashamedly bare-chested—the vulnerability of yesterday nothing but a distant memory. His black eyes glittered with displeasure as he saw her, and his voice was cool.

'Ah, Izzy. At last.'

'Is something wrong?' she asked.

'Damned right there is.'

A tall, bespectacled man detached himself from the group, extending his hand and introducing himself as the consultant. 'You're his partner?' he asked Isobel, as he glanced down at the overnight bag she was carrying.

Isobel went bright red, and she couldn't miss the narrow-eyed look which Tariq angled in her direction. But for some reason she was glad that she wasn't the same wild-haired scarecrow she'd been in the middle of the night. That she'd taken the care to wash and tame her hair and put on her favourite russet-coloured jacket.

Just because the Sheikh never looked at her in the way he looked at other women it didn't mean she was immune to a little masculine attention from time to time, did it? She gave the doctor a quick smile. 'No, Doctor. I'm Isobel Mulholland. The Sheikh's assistant.'

'Well, perhaps you could manage to talk some sense into your boss, Isobel,' said the consultant, meeting her eyes with a resigned expression. 'He's had a nasty bang to the head and a general shock to the system—but he seems to think that he can walk out of here and carry on as normal.' The doctor continued to hold her gaze. 'It sounds like a punishing regime at the best of times, but especially so in the circumstances. Unless he agrees to take things easy for the next week—'

'I can't,' interrupted Tariq testily, wondering if his perception had been altered by the bump on the head he'd received. Was the doctor *flirting with Isobel?* And was she—the woman he'd never known as anything other than a brisk and efficient machine—*flirting back?* He had never found her in the least bit attractive himself, but Tariq was unused to being overlooked for another man, and his mouth thinned as he subjected the medic to an icy look. 'I need to fly to the States tomorrow.'

'That's where you're wrong. You need rest,' contradicted the consultant. 'Complete rest. Away from work and the world—and away from the media, who have been plaguing my office all morning. You've been driving yourself too hard and you need to recuperate. Otherwise I'll have no alternative but to keep you in.'

'You can't keep me in against my will,' objected Tariq.

Isobel recognised that a stand-off between the two men was about to be reached—and she knew that Tariq would refuse to back down if it got to that stage. Diplomatically, she offered the consultant another polite smile. 'Does he need any particular medical care, Doctor?'

'Will you stop talking about me as if I'm not here?' growled Tariq.

'Just calm and quiet observation,' said the doctor. 'And a guarantee that he won't go anywhere near his office for at least seven days.'

Isobel's mind began to race. He could go to a clinic, yes—but even the most discreet of clinics could never be relied on to be *that* discreet, could they? Especially when they were dealing with billionaire patients who were being hunted by the tabloids. Tariq didn't need expensive clinics where people would no doubt seek to exploit his wealth and influence. He needed that thing which always seemed to elude him.

Peace.

She thought about the strange flash of vulnerability she'd seen on his face and an idea began to form in her mind.

'I have a little cottage in the countryside,' she said slowly, looking straight into a pair of black and disbelieving eyes. 'You could come and stay there for a week, if you like. My mother used to be a nurse, and I picked up some basic first aid from her. I could keep my eye on you, Tariq.'

CHAPTER TWO

'WHERE the hell are you going, Izzy?'

For a moment Isobel didn't answer Tariq's growled question as she turned the small car into a narrow country lane edged with budding hedgerows. Why couldn't he just settle down and relax—and be grateful she'd managed to get him out of the hospital? Maybe even sit back and appreciate the beauty of the spring day instead of haranguing her all the time?

It wasn't until she was bowling along at a steady pace that she risked a quick glance and saw the still-dreadful pallor of his face, which showed no signs of shifting. He was in *pain,* she reminded herself—and besides, he was a man who rarely expressed gratitude.

Already she'd had to bite back her words several times that morning. They had left by a staff exit at the back of the hospital, and although he had initially refused to travel in a wheelchair she had persuaded him that it would help elude any waiting press. Which of course, it had. The photographers were looking for the muscular stride of a powerful sheikh—not a man being pushed along by a woman. She remembered her mother telling her that nobody ever looked at people in wheelchairs—how society was often too busy to care about those who were not able-bodied. And it seemed that her mother was right.

'You know very well where I'm going,' she answered calmly. 'To my cottage in the country, where you are going to recuperate after your crash. That was the agreement we made with the doctor before he would agree to discharge you. Remember?'

He made a small sound of displeasure beneath his breath. His head was throbbing, his throat felt as dry as parchment, and now Izzy was being infuriatingly *stubborn*. 'That's the doctor you were flirting with so outrageously?' he questioned coolly.

Isobel's eyes narrowed as she acknowledged her boss's accusation. In truth, she'd been so worried about *him* that she'd barely given a thought to the crinkly-eyed consultant. But even if she *had* fallen in love at first sight and decided to slip the doctor her phone number—well, it was none of Tariq's business. Wasn't she doing enough for him already, without him attempting to police her private life for her?

'And what if I was?' she retorted.

He shrugged. 'I would have thought that extremely unprofessional behaviour on his part.'

'I hardly think that you're in any position to pass judgement on flirting,' she murmured.

Tariq drummed his fingers against one tense thigh. It was not the response he'd been expecting. A firm assertion that the doctor had been wasting his time would have been infinitely more desirable. Isobel was resolutely single, and that was the way he liked it. It meant that she could devote herself to *his* needs and be there whenever *he* wanted her.

'I thought you only told him all that stuff about taking me to your cottage to get him off my back,' he objected.

'But that would have been dishonest.'

'Do you always have to be so damned *moral?*'

'One of us has to have morals.'

His eyes narrowed. 'Is that supposed to be a criticism?'

'No, Tariq,' she answered calmly. 'It's merely an observation.'

He stared at her set profile and inexplicably began to notice the way the pale spring sunshine was picking out the lights in her hair, turning it a glowing shade of amber. Had the doctor also noticed its subtle fire? he wondered. Would that explain his behaviour? 'I don't know why you're dragging me out to the back of beyond,' he said, 'when I can rest perfectly well at home.'

'In central London?' She gave a dry laugh. 'With the press baying at your door like hounds and all your ex-girlfriends lining up to offer to come and mop your brow for you? I don't think so. You'll be much safer at my cottage. Anyway, it's a done deal. I've informed the office that you'll be incommunicado for a week, and that all calls are to come through me. Fiona in the PR office is perfectly capable of running things until we get back. I've had your housekeeper pack a week's worth of clothes, which are being couriered down. And I haven't told anybody about your exact whereabouts.'

'My brother—'

'Except for your brother,' she concurred, remembering the brief conversation she'd had earlier that day with the ruler of Khayarzah. 'I telephoned the palace and spoke to the King myself—told him that you're on the mend but that you needed to recuperate. He wanted you flown to Khayarzah, but I said that you would be fine with me.' She shot him a glance. 'That was the right thing to do, wasn't it?'

'I suppose so,' he answered moodily, but as usual she had done exactly the right thing. The last thing he needed was the formality of palace life—with all the strictures that came with it. He'd done his level best to escape from the attendant attention which came with being the brother of the King—a role which had been thrust on him when his brother had suddenly inherited the crown. A role which had threatened his freedom—something he had always guarded jealously. Because wasn't his freedom the only good thing to have emerged from the terrible isolation of his childhood?

He fixed her with a cool and curious stare. 'You seem to have it all worked out, Izzy.'

'Well, that's what you pay me for.' She glanced in the driving mirror and let a speedy white van overtake them before starting to speak again. 'Do you want to tell me what happened? About why one of the most careful drivers I know should crash his car?'

Tariq closed his eyes. Wasn't it frustrating that a split-second decision could impact so dramatically on your life? If he hadn't been beguiled by a pair of blue eyes and a dynamite body then he wouldn't be facing the rather grim prospect of being stuck in some remote cottage with his assistant for a week.

'I went for dinner with a woman,' he said.

'No—' Isobel started to say something and then changed her mind, but Tariq seized on her swallowed words like a cat capturing a mouse.

His thick lashes parted by a fraction. 'No what, Izzy?'

'It doesn't matter.'

'Oh, but it does,' he answered stubbornly.

'I was about to say no change there. You having dinner with a woman is hardly remarkable, Tariq. Blonde, was she?'

'Actually, she was.' Reluctantly, his lips curved into a smile. Sometimes Izzy was so damned sharp he was surprised she didn't cut herself. Maybe that was what less attractive women did—they made up for their shortcomings by developing a more sophisticated sense of humour. 'But she wasn't all she seemed to be.'

'Not a transvestite, I hope?'

'Very funny.' But despite the smile which her flippant comment produced Tariq was irritated with himself. He had been stressed out, and had intended to relax by playing poker until the small hours. He hadn't really been in the mood for any kind of liaison, or the effort of chatting someone up. But the woman had been very beautiful, and he'd found himself inviting her for a late dinner. And then she had started to question him. Wanting to know the kind of things which suggested that she might have done more than a little background research on him.

Tariq had some rules which were entirely his own.

He didn't like being interrogated.

He didn't trust people who knew too much about him.

And he never slept with a woman on a first date.

At heart, he was a deeply old-fashioned man, with plenty of contradictory values. For him sex had always been laughably easy—yet he didn't respect a woman who let him too close, too soon. Especially as he had a very short attention span when it came to the opposite sex. He liked the slow burn of anticipation—to prolong the ache of desire until it became unbearable. So when the blonde had made it very clear that she was his for the taking—some primitive sense of prudery had reared its head. Who wanted something which was so easily obtained? With a jaded yawn, he had declined her offer and reached for his jacket.

And that was when the woman's story had come blurting out. It seemed that it hadn't been fate which had brought her into his life, but cunning and subterfuge.

'She was a journalist,' he bit out. He'd been so angry with himself because he hadn't seen through her flimsy cover. Furious that he had fallen for one of the oldest tricks of all. He'd stormed out, wondering if he was losing his touch, and for those few seconds when his attention had wandered so had had his powerful sports car. 'She wanted the inside story on the takeover bid,' he finished.

Isobel shrugged as her little car took a bend in the road. 'Well, if you *will* try and buy into the Premier League, what do you expect? You know the English are crazy about football—and it's a really big deal if some power-hungry Sheikh adds a major team to his portfolio.'

'There's nothing wrong with being hungry for power, Izzy.'

'Only if it becomes addictive,' she countered.

'You think I'm a power junkie?'

'That's not for me to say.'

His black eyes narrowed. 'I notice you didn't deny it, though.'

'I'm glad you're paying attention to what I say, Tariq.'

With a small click of irritation, he attempted, without much success, to stretch his legs. Some lurid looking air-freshener in the shape of a blue daisy hung from the driving mirror and danced infuriatingly in front of the windscreen. Other than the occasional childhood ride on a camel in his homeland, he could never remember enduring such an uncomfortable form of transport as this. Rather longingly, he thought about the dented bonnet of his smooth and gleaming sports car and wondered how long before it would be roadworthy again.

'Is your cottage as cramped as your car?' he demanded.

'You don't like my car?'

'Not really. I don't like second-hand cars which don't go above fifty.'

'Then why don't you give me a pay rise?' she suggested sweetly. 'And I'll buy myself a newer one.'

For a moment Tariq acknowledged the brief flicker of discord which made his pulse quicken. Wasn't it strange how a little tension between a man and a woman could instantly begin to heat a man's blood and make him start thinking of…

But the smile left his face as he realised that this was *Izzy* he was about to start fantasising about. Safe and sensible Izzy. The plain stalwart of his office—and the very last candidate for any erotic thoughts. So how was it that he suddenly found his attention riveted on a pair of slender thighs which were outlined with delectable precision beneath the blue of her denim skirt?

With an effort, he dragged his gaze away and settled back in the seat. 'I pay you enough already—as well you know,' he said. 'How far is it?'

'Far enough,' said Isobel softly, 'for you to close your eyes and sleep.' *And stop annoying me with your infuriating comments.*

'I'm not sleepy.'

'Sure?'

'Quite sure,' he mumbled, but something in her voice was oddly soothing, so he found himself yawning—and seconds later he was fast asleep.

Isobel drove in a silence punctuated only by the low, steady sound of Tariq's breathing. She tried to concentrate on her driving and on the new green buds which were pushing through the hedgerows—but it wasn't easy. Her attention kept wandering and she felt oddly light-headed. She kept telling herself it was because her usual routine had been thrown out of kilter—and not because of the disturbing proximity of her boss.

But that wouldn't have been true. Something had happened to her and she couldn't work out what it was. Why should she suddenly start feeling self-conscious and *peculiar* in Tariq's company? Why couldn't she seem to stop her eyes from straying to the powerful shafts of his thighs and then drifting upwards to the narrow jut of his hips?

She shook her head. She'd been alone with Tariq many, many times before. She had shared train, plane and car journeys with him on various business trips. But never like this. Not in such cramped and humble confines, with him fast asleep beside her, his legs spread out in front of him. Almost as if they were any normal couple, just driving along.

Impatiently, she shook her head.

Normal? That was the last adjective which could ever be applied to Tariq. He was a royal sheikh from the ancient House of Khayarzah and one of the wealthiest men on the planet.

Sometimes it still seemed incredible to Isobel that

someone like her should have ended up working so closely for such a powerful man. She could tell that people were often surprised when she told them what she did for a living. That he who could have anyone should have chosen her. What did *she* have that a thousand more well-connected women didn't have? That was what everyone always wanted to know.

Deep down, she suspected it was because he trusted her in a way that he trusted few people. And why did he trust her? Hard to say. Probably because she had met him when he was young—at school—before the true extent of his power and position had really sunk in. Before he'd realised the influence he wielded.

She'd been just ten at the time—a solitary and rather serious child. Her mother, Anna, had been the school nurse at one of England's most prestigious boarding schools—a job she'd been lucky to get since it provided a place to live as well as a steady income. Anna was a single mother and her daughter Isobel illegitimate. Times had changed, and not having a father no longer carried any stigma, but it certainly had back then—back in the day.

Isobel had borne the brunt of it, of course. She remembered the way she'd always flinched with embarrassment whenever the question had been asked: *What does your father do?* There had been a thousand ways she had sought to answer without giving away the shaming fact that she *didn't actually know.*

As a consequence, she'd always felt slightly *less than*—a feeling which hadn't been helped by growing up surrounded by some of the wealthiest children in the world. She'd been educated among them, but she had never really been one of them—those pampered products of the privileged classes.

But Tariq had been different from all the other pupils. His olive skin and black eyes had made him stand out like a handful of sparkling jewels thrown down onto a sheet of plain white paper. Sent to the west to be educated by his father, he had excelled in everything he'd done. He'd swum and ridden and played tennis—and he spoke five languages with native fluency.

Sometimes, Isobel had gazed at him with wistful wonder from afar. Had watched as he was surrounded by natural blondes with tiny-boned bodies and swish flats in Chelsea.

Until the day he had spoken to her and made a lonely little girl's day.

He'd have been about seventeen at the time, and had come to the sanatorium to ask about a malaria injection for a forthcoming trip he was taking. Her mother had been busy with one of the other pupils and had asked Isobel to keep the young Prince entertained.

Initially Isobel had been tongue-tied—wondering what on earth she could say to him. But she couldn't just leave him looking rather impatiently at his golden wristwatch, could she? Why, her mother might get into trouble for daring to keep the young royal waiting.

Shyly, she had asked him about his homeland. At first he had frowned—as if her question was an intrusion. But a brief and assessing look had followed, and then he had sat down so that he was on her level before starting to talk. The precise words she had long forgotten, but she would never forget the dreamy way he had spoken of desert sands like fine gold and rivers like streams of silver. And then, when her mother had appeared—looking a little flustered—he had immediately switched to the persona of confident royal pupil. He hadn't said another word to her—but Isobel had never forgotten that brief encounter.

It had been over a decade later before their paths crossed again. She had gone back to the school for the opening of a magnificent extension to the library and Tariq had been there, still surrounded by adoring women. For one brief moment Isobel had looked at him with adult eyes. Had registered that he was still as gorgeous as he was unobtainable and that her schoolgirl crush should sensibly die a death. With a resigned little shrug of her shoulders she had turned away and put him right out of her mind as of that moment.

The new library was fabulous, with softly gleaming carved wooden panels. Tooled leather tables sat at its centre, and the long, leaded arched windows looked out onto the cool beauty of the north gardens.

By then Isobel had been a secretary—working in a dusty office for a rather dry bunch of lawyers in London. It hadn't been the most exciting work in the world, but it had been well paid, and had provided her with the security she had always craved.

There'd been no one in the library that she knew well enough to go up and talk to, but she'd been determined to enjoy her time there, because secretly she'd been delighted to get an invitation to the prestigious opening. Just because she'd been educated at the school free, it didn't mean she'd been overlooked! She'd drunk a cup of tea and then begun to look at the books, noting with interest that there was a whole section on Khayarzah. Picking up a beautifully bound volume, she'd begun to flick through the pages, and had soon been lost in the pictures and descriptions of the land which Tariq had once made come alive with his words.

She'd just got to a bit about the source of the Jamanah River when she'd heard a deep voice behind her.

'You seem very engrossed in that book.'

And, turning round, she'd found herself imprisoned in the Sheikh's curious gaze. She'd thought that his face was harder and colder than she remembered—and that there was a certain air of detachment about him. But then Isobel recalled the sixth-former who'd been so kind to her, and had smiled.

'That's because it's a very engrossing book,' she said. 'Though I'm surprised there's such a big section on your country.'

'Really?' A pair of jet eyebrows was elevated. 'One of the benefits of donating a library is that you get to choose some of its contents.'

Isobel blinked. '*You* donated the new library?'

'Of course.' His voice took on a faintly cynical air. 'Didn't you realise that wealthy old boys—particularly foreign ones—are expected to play benefactor at some point in their lives?'

'No, I didn't.'

Afterwards, Isobel thought that his question might have been some sort of test—to see if she was one of those people who were impressed by wealth. And if that *was* the case then she'd probably passed it. Because she genuinely didn't care about money. She had enough for her needs and that was plenty. What had her mother always told her? *Don't aim too high; just high enough.*

'I just wanted to know if it was as beautiful as...' Her words tailed off. As if he could *possibly* be interested!

But he was looking at her curiously, as if he *was* interested.

'As beautiful as what?'

She swallowed. 'As the way you described it. You once told me all about Khayarzah. You were very…passionate about it. You said the sand was like fine gold and the rivers like streams of silver. You probably don't remember.'

Tariq stared at her, as if he was trying to place her, but shook his head.

'No, I don't remember,' he admitted, and then, as he glanced up to see a determined-looking blonde making her way towards them, he took Isobel's elbow. 'So why don't you refresh my memory for me?' And he led her away to a quieter section of the room.

And that was that. An unexpected meeting between two people who had both felt like outsiders within the privileged walls of an English public school. What was more it seemed that Tariq happened to have a need, and that Isobel could be just the person to answer that need. He was looking for someone to be his assistant. Someone he could talk to without her being fazed by who he was and what he represented. Someone he could trust.

The salary he was offering made it madness for her even to consider refusing, so Isobel accepted his offer and quickly realised that no job description in the world could have prepared her for working for *him.*

He wanted honesty, yes—but he also demanded deference, as and when it suited him.

He was fair, but he was also a powerful sheikh who had untold wealth at his fingertips—so he could also be highly unreasonable, too.

And he was sexy. As sexy as any man was ever likely to be. Everyone said so—even Isobel's more feminist friends, who disapproved of him. But Isobel's strength was that she simply refused to see it. After that meeting in the library she had trained herself to be immune to his appeal as if she was training for a marathon. Even if she considered herself to be in his league—which she didn't—she still wouldn't have been foolish enough to fancy him.

Because men like Tariq were trouble—too aware of their power over the opposite sex and not afraid to use it. She'd watched as women who fell in love with him were discarded once he'd tired of them. And she knew from her own background how lives could be ruined if passion was allowed to rule the roost. Hadn't her mother bitterly regretted falling for a charmer like Tariq? Telling her that the brief liaison had affected her whole life?

No, he was definitely not on Isobel's wish-list of men. His strong, muscular body and hard, hawkish features didn't fill her with longing, but with an instinctive wariness which had always served her well.

Because she wouldn't have lasted five minutes—let alone five years—if she had lost her heart to the Sheikh.

She steered the car up a narrow lane and came to a halt outside her beloved little cottage. The March sunshine was clear and pale, illuminating the purple, white and yellow crocuses which were pushing through the earth. She loved this time of year, with all its new beginnings and endless possibilities. Opening the car door a fraction, she could hear birds tweeting their jubilant celebration of springtime—but still Tariq didn't stir.

She turned to look at him—at the ebony arcs of his feathered lashes which were the only soft component to make up his formidable face. She had never seen him asleep before, and it was like looking at a very different man. The hard planes and angles of his features threw shadows over his olive skin, and for once his sensual lips were relaxed. Once again she saw an unfamiliar trace of vulnerability etched on his features, and once again she felt that little stab of awareness at her heart.

He was so *still,* she thought wonderingly. Remarkably still for a man who rarely stopped. Who drove himself remorselessly in the way that successful men always did. Why, it seemed almost a shame to wake him...and to have him face the reality of his convalescence in her humble home.

Racking her brain, she thought back to how she'd left the place last weekend, and realised that there was no fresh food or milk. Stuff she would normally have brought down with her from London.

Reaching out her hand, she touched his shoulder lightly—but his eyelashes moved instantly, the black eyes suspicious and alert as they snapped open.

For a moment Tariq stayed perfectly still, his memory filtering back in jigsaw pieces. What was he doing sitting in an uncomfortably cramped and strange car, while Izzy frowned down at him, her breathing slightly quickened and her amber eyes dark with concern?

And then he remembered. She had offered to play nursemaid for the next week—just not the kind of nursemaid which would have been *his* preference. His mouth hardened as he dispelled an instant fantasy of a woman with creamy curves busting out of a little uniform which ill concealed the black silk stockings beneath. Because Isobel was not that woman. And under the circumstances wasn't that best?

'We're here!' said Isobel brightly, even though her heart had inexplicably started thudding at some dangerous and unknown quality she'd read in his black eyes. 'Welcome to my home.'

CHAPTER THREE

'CAREFUL,' warned Isobel.

'Please don't state the obvious,' Tariq snapped, as he bent his head to avoid the low front door.

'I was only trying to help,' she protested, as he walked straight past her.

Stepping into the cluttered sitting room was no better, and Tariq quickly discovered that the abundance of overhanging beams was nothing short of a health hazard. 'I've already had one knock to the head, and I don't particularly want another,' he growled. 'Why is your damned ceiling so low?'

'Because men didn't stand at over six feet when these houses were built!' she retorted, thinking that he had to be the most ungrateful man ever to have drawn breath. Here she was, putting herself out by giving him housespace for a week, and all he could do was come out with a litany of complaints.

But some of her exasperation dissolved as she closed the front door, so that the two of them were enclosed in a room which up until that moment she had always thought of as a safe and cosy sanctuary. But not any more. Suddenly it didn't seem safe at all...

She felt hot blood begin to flood through her veins—

because the reality of having Tariq standing here was having a bizarre effect on her senses. Had the dimensions magically shrunk? Or was it just his towering physique which dwarfed everything else around him?

Even in jeans and the soft swathing of a grey cashmere sweater he seemed to exude a charisma which drew the eye like nothing else. His faded jeans were stretched over powerful thighs and the sweater hinted at honed muscle beneath. Somehow he managed to make her cottage look like a prop from Toytown, and the thick and solid walls suddenly seemed insubstantial. Come to think of it, didn't she feel a little insubstantial herself?

She remembered that uncomfortable feeling of awareness which had come over her in the hospital—when she'd looked down at him and something inside her had melted. It was as if in that moment she had suddenly given herself permission to see him as other women saw him—and the impact of that had rocked her. And now it was rocking her all over again. Something about the way he was standing there was making her heart slam hard against her ribcage, and an aching feeling began to tug at her belly.

Isobel swallowed, willing this temporary madness to subside. Because acknowledging Tariq's charisma was the last thing she needed right now. Arrogant playboys were not number one on her list of emotional requirements. And even if they were…as if he would ever look at a woman like *her*.

She flashed him a quick smile, even as she became aware of the peculiar prickle of her breasts. 'Look, why don't you sit down and I'll make you some tea?'

'I don't want any tea,' he said. 'But I'd quite like to

avoid getting frostbite. It's absolutely freezing in here. Give me some matches and I'll light a fire.'

Isobel shook her head. 'You aren't supposed to be lighting fires. In fact, you aren't supposed to be doing anything but resting. I can manage perfectly well—so will you please sit down on the sofa and put your feet up and let me look after you?'

Tariq's eyes narrowed as her protective command washed over him. His first instinct was to resist. He wasn't used to *care* from the fairer sex. His experience of women usually involved the rapid removal of their clothing and them gasping out their pleasure when he touched them. Big eyes clouded with concern tended to be outside his experience.

'And if I don't?' he challenged softly.

Their gazes clashed in a way which made Isobel's stomach perform a peculiar little flip. She saw the mocking curve of his lips and suddenly she felt almost *weak*— as if she were the invalid, not him. Clamping down the sudden rise of longing, she shook her head—because she was damned if he was going to manipulate her the way other women let him manipulate *them*. 'I don't think you're in any position to object,' she answered coolly. 'And if you did I could always threaten to hand my notice in.'

'You wouldn't do that, Izzy.'

'Oh, wouldn't I?' she returned fiercely, because now she could see a hint of that awful pallor returning to his face, and a horrifying thought occurred to her. Yes, her mother had been a nurse, and she had learned lots of basic first aid through her. She had managed to convince the hospital doctor that she could cope. But what if she had taken on more than she could handle? What if Tariq began to have side-effects from his head injury? She thought about the hospital leaflet in her handbag and decided that she'd better consult it. 'Now, will you please *sit down?*'

Unexpectedly, Tariq gave a low laugh. 'You can be a fierce little tiger at times, can't you?'

Something about his very obvious approval made her cheeks grow warm with pleasure. 'I can if I need to be.'

'Okay, you win.' Sinking down onto a chintzy and over-stuffed sofa, he batted her a sardonic look. 'Is that better, *Nurse?*'

Trying not to laugh, Isobel nodded. 'Marginally. Do you think you could just try sitting there quietly while I light the fire?'

'I can try.'

Tariq leaned back against a heap of cushions and watched as she busied herself with matches and kindling. Funny, really—he'd never really pictured Izzy in a cottage which was distinctly chocolate-boxy despite the sub-zero temperatures. Not that he'd given very much thought at all as to how his assistant lived her life.

Stifling a yawn, he looked around. The sitting room had those tiny windows which didn't let in very much light, and a big, recessed fireplace—the kind you saw on the front of Christmas cards. She was crouching down in front of the grate, and he watched as she began to blow on the flames to coax them into life. He found his eyes drawn to the denim skirt, which now stretched tightly over the curves of her buttocks.

He swallowed down a sudden, debilitating leap of desire which made him harden in a way he hadn't been expecting. In five years of close contact with his highly efficient assistant he couldn't remember ever noticing her bottom before. And it was actually a rather fine bottom. Firm and high and beautifully rounded. The kind of bottom which a man liked to cup in the palms of his hands as he...

'What?' Isobel turned round and frowned.

'I didn't...' Tariq swallowed. What the hell was going on? Did bumps to the head make men lose their senses, so that they started imagining all kinds of inappropriate things? 'I didn't say anything.'

'But you made a funny sort of noise.' Her eyes narrowed as she looked at him. 'Are you all right? Your eyes have gone all glazed.'

'Are you surprised?' Shifting his position, Tariq glared at her, willing his erection to subside. 'I've just had to endure your driving.'

Isobel turned back to the now leaping flames, an unseen smile playing around her lips. If he was jumping down her throat like that, then there couldn't be very much wrong with him.

She waited until the fire was properly alight and then went into the kitchen and made his favourite mint tea—bringing it back into the sitting room on a tray set with bone china cups and a jar of farm honey.

To her relief, she could see that he had taken her at her word. He'd kicked off his hand-made Italian shoes and was lying stretched out on the sofa, despite it being slightly too small to accommodate his lengthy frame. His thick black hair was outlined by a chintz cushion and his powerful thighs were splayed indolently against the faded velvet. It made an incongruous image, she realised—to see the *über*-masculine Sheikh in such a domestic setting as this.

She poured tea for them both, added honey to his,

and put it down a small table beside him, her gaze straying to his face as she sat on the floor beside the fire.
Tariq was known for his faintly unshaven buccaneering
look, but today the deep shadowing which outlined the
hard definition of his jaw made him look like a study
in brooding testosterone.

Now it was Isobel's turn to feel vulnerable. That
faint butterflies-in-the-stomach feeling was back, big-
time. And so was that sudden sensitive prickling of her
breasts. She swallowed. 'How are you feeling?'

His eyes narrowed. 'Will you stop talking to me as
if I'm an invalid?'

'But that's what you are, Tariq—otherwise you
wouldn't be here, would you? Just put my mind at rest.
I'm not asking you to divulge the secrets of your heart—
just answer the question.'

For the first time he became aware of the faint shadows beneath her eyes. She must be tired, he realised suddenly, and frowned. Hadn't he woken her at the crack of
dawn yesterday? Called her and known she would come
running to his aid without a second thought—because
that was what she always did? Safe, reliable Izzy, who
was always there when he needed her—often before
he even realised he did. It wasn't an observation which
would have normally occurred to him, and the novelty
of that made him consider her question instead of batting it away with his habitual impatience.

Oddly—apart from the lessening ache in his head and
the woolly feeling which came from his having been in-
active for over a day—he felt strangely relaxed. Usually
he was alert and driven, restlessly looking ahead to the
next challenge. He was also constantly on his guard,
knowing that his royal blood made him a target for all

kinds of social climbers. Or journalists masquerading as dinner-dates.

Since his brother had unexpectedly acceded to the throne it had grown worse—placing him firmly in the public eye. He was bitterly aware that his words were always listened to, often distorted and then repeated—so he used them with caution.

Yet right now he felt a rush of unfamiliar *contentment* which was completely alien to him. For the first time in his adult life he found himself alone in a confined space with a woman who wasn't intent on removing his clothes....

'I have a slight ache in my...' he shifted his position as she tucked her surprisingly long legs beneath her and he felt another sharp kick of awareness '...head. But other than that I feel okay.'

The gleam in his black eyes was making Isobel feel uncomfortable. She wished he'd stop *looking* at her like that. Rather unnecessarily, she gave the fire a quick poke. 'Good.'

Tariq sipped at his tea, noting the sudden tension in her shoulders. Was she feeling it too? he wondered. This powerful sexual awareness which was simmering in the air around them?

With an effort, he pushed it from his mind and sought refuge in the conventional. 'I didn't realise you had a place like this. I thought you lived in town.'

Isobel laid the poker back down in the grate, his question making her realise the one-sided quality of their relationship. She knew all about *his* life—but he knew next to nothing about hers, did he?

'I do live in town. I just keep this as a weekend place—which is a bit of a luxury. I really ought to sell it and buy myself something larger than the shoebox I currently inhabit in London, but I can't quite bring my-self to let it go. My mother worked hard to buy it, you see. She lived rent-free at the school, of course, and when she retired she moved here.' She read the question in his eyes, took a deep breath and faced it full-on. 'She died six years ago and left it to me.'

'And what about your father?'

All her old defensiveness sprang into place. 'What about him?'

'You never talk about him.'

'That's because you never ask.'

'No. You're right. I don't.' And the reason he never asked was because he wasn't particularly interested in the private lives of his staff. The less you knew about the people who worked for you, the less complication all round.

But surely these circumstances were unusual enough to allow him to break certain rules? And didn't Izzy's hesitancy alert his interest? Arouse his natural hunter instincts? Tariq leaned back against the pillow of his folded elbows and studied her. 'I'm asking now.'

Isobel met the curiosity in his eyes. If it had been anyone else she might have told them to mind their own business, or used the evasive tactics she'd employed all her life. She was protective of her private life and her past—and hated being judged or pitied. But that was the trouble with having a personal conversation with your boss—you weren't exactly on equal terms, were you? And Tariq wasn't just *any* boss. His authority was en-riched with the sense of entitlement which came with his princely title and his innate belief that he was always right. Would he be shocked to learn of her illegitimacy?

She shrugged her shoulders, as if what she was about to say didn't matter. 'I don't know my father.'

'What do you mean, you don't know him?'

'Just that. I never saw him, nor met him. To me, he was just a man my mother had a relationship with. Only it turned out that he was actually married to someone else at the time.'

He narrowed his eyes. 'So what happened?'

She remembered all the different emotions which had crossed her mother's face when she had recounted her tale. Hurt. Resentment. And a deep and enduring sense of anger and betrayal. Men were the enemy, who could so easily walk away from their responsibilities, Anna Mulholland had said. Had that negativity brushed off on her only daughter and contributed to Isobel's own poor record with men? Maybe it had—for she'd never let anyone close enough to really start to care about them.

'He didn't want to know about a baby,' she answered slowly. 'Said he didn't want anything to do with it. My mother thought it was shock making him talk that way. She gave him a few days to think about it. Only when she tried to contact him again—he'd gone.'

'Gone?' Tariq raised his eyebrows. 'Gone where?'

'That's the whole point—she never knew. He'd completely vanished.' She met the look of disbelief in his eyes and shook her head. 'It was only a quarter of a century ago, but it was a different kind of world back then. There were no computers you could use to track people down. No Facebook or cellphones. A man and his wife could just disappear off the face of the earth and you would never see them again.'

Tariq's frown deepened. 'So he never saw you?'

'Nope. Not once. He doesn't even know I exist,' she

answered, as if she didn't care—and sometimes she actually managed to convince herself that she didn't. Wasn't it better to have an absent father rather than one who resented you, or didn't match up to your expectations? But deep down Isobel knew that wasn't the whole story. There was always a bitter ache in her heart when she thought about the parent she'd never had.

For a moment Tariq tensed, as an unwilling sense of identification washed over him. Her childhood sounded sterile and lonely—and wasn't that territory he was painfully familiar with? The little boy sent far away from home to endure a rigid system where his royal blood made him the victim of envy? And, like her, he had never known what it was to be part of a 'normal' family.

Suddenly, he found his voice dipping in empathy. 'That's a pretty tough thing to happen,' he said.

Isobel heard the softness of his tone but shook her head, determined to shield herself from his unexpected sympathy—because sympathy made you weak. It made regret and yearning wash over you. Made you start wishing things could have been different. And everyone knew you could never rewrite the past.

'It is what it is. Some people have to contend with far worse. My childhood was comfortable and safe—and you can't knock something like that. Now, would you like some more tea before it gets cold?' she questioned briskly.

He could tell from the brightness in her voice that she wanted to change the subject, and suddenly he found he was relieved. It had been his mistake to encourage too much introspection—especially about the past. Because didn't it open up memories which did no one any good?

Memories which were best avoided because they took you to dark places?

He shook his head. 'No thanks. Just show me which bathroom you want me to use.'

'Right.' Isobel hesitated. Why hadn't she thought of this? 'The thing is that there's only one bathroom, I'm afraid.' She bit her lip. 'We're going to have to...well, share.'

There was a pause. 'Share?' he repeated.

She met the disbelief in his eyes. He's a *prince,* she reminded herself. He won't be used to sharing and making do. But it might do him some good to see how the other half lived—to see there were places other than the luxurious penthouses and palaces he'd always called home.

'My cottage is fairly basic, but it's comfortable,' she said proudly. 'I've never had the need or the money to incorporate an *en-suite* bathroom—so I'm afraid you'll just have to get used to it. Now, would you like me to show you where you'll be sleeping?'

Tariq gave a mirthless smile, acknowledging that it was the first time he'd ever been asked that particular question without the involvement of some kind of foreplay. Wordlessly he nodded as he rose from the sofa to follow her out into the hall and up a very old wooden staircase. The trouble was that her movements showcased her bottom even more than before. Because this time he was closer—and every mounting step made the blue denim cling like honey to each magnificent globe.

How could he have been so blind never to have noticed it before? His gaze travelled downwards. Or to have registered the fact that her legs were really very shapely—the ankles slim enough to be circled by his finger and his thumb…?

'This is the bathroom,' Isobel was saying. 'And right next door is your room. See?'

She pushed open a door and Tariq stepped inside and looked around, glad to be distracted by something other than the erotic nature of his thoughts.

It was a room like no room he'd ever seen. A modestly sized iron bedstead was covered with flower-sprigged bedlinen, and on top of one of the pillows sat a faded teddy bear. In the corner was an old-fashioned dressing table and a dark, rickety-looking wardrobe—other than that, the room was bare.

Yet as Tariq walked over to the window he could see that the view was incredible—overlooking nothing but unadulterated countryside. Hedgerows lined the narrow lane, and primroses grew in thick lemon clusters along the banks. Beyond that lay field after field—until eventually the land met the sky. There was absolutely no sound, he realised. Not a car, nor a plane—nor the distant trill of someone's phone.

The silence was all-enveloping, and a strange sense of peace settled on him. It crept over his skin like the first sun after a long winter and he gave a sigh of unfamiliar contentment. Turning around, he became aware that Izzy had walked over to the window to join him. And she was looking up at him, her eyes wide and faintly uncertain.

'Do you think you could be comfortable here?' she questioned.

Contentment forgotten now, he watched as she bit her lip and her teeth left behind a tiny indentation. He saw the sudden gleam as the tip of her tongue moistened the spot. Her tawny eyes were slitted against the sunlight which illuminated the magnificent Titian fire of her hair. Wasn't it peculiar that before today he'd never really noticed that her hair was such an amazing colour? And that, coupled with the proximity of her newly discovered curvaceous body, made a powerful impulse come over him.

He forgot that she was sensible Isobel—the reliable and rather sexless assistant who organised his life for him. He forgot everything other than the aching throb at his groin, which was tempting him with an insistence he was finding difficult to ignore. He wanted to kiss her. To plunder those unpainted lips with a fierce kind of hunger. To cup those delicious globes of her bottom and find if they were covered with cotton or lace. And then...

He felt the rapid escalation of desire as his sexual fantasy took on a vivid life of its own and the deep pulse of hunger began a primitive beat in his blood. For a moment he let its tempting warmth steal into his body, and he almost gave in to its powerful lure.

But Tariq prided himself on his formidable willpower, and his ability to turn his back on temptation. Because the truth was that there wasn't a woman in the world who couldn't be replaced.

What would be the point of seducing Isobel when the potential fall-out from that seduction could have far-reaching consequences? She'd probably fall in love with him—as women so often did—and when he ended it, what then?

When she'd told him about her father he'd seen a streak of steel and determination which might indicate that she wasn't a total marshmallow—but still he couldn't risk it. She was far more valuable to him as a member of staff than as a temporary lover.

He saw that she was still waiting for an answer to her question, the anxious hostess eager for reassurance, and he gave her a careless smile. 'I think it will be perfectly *adequate* for my needs,' he answered.

Isobel nodded. Not the most heartfelt of thanks, it was true—but who cared? She was feeling so disorientated that she could barely think straight. Had she imagined that almost *electric* feeling which had sizzled between them just now? When something unknown and tantalising had shimmered in the air around them, making her blood grow thick with desire? When she'd longed for him to pull her into his arms and just *kiss* her?

Apprehension skittered over her skin as she tried to tell herself that she didn't find Tariq attractive. She *didn't*. Her innate fear of feckless men had always protected her from his undeniable charisma.

So what had happened to that precious immunity now? Was it because they were in *her* home, and on *her* territory instead of his, that she felt so shockingly vulnerable in his presence? Or because she'd been stupid enough to blurt out parts of her life which she'd always kept tucked away, and in so doing had opened up a vulnerable side of herself?

Suddenly she was achingly aware of his proximity. Every taut sinew of his powerful body seemed to tantalise her and send a thousand questions racing through her mind. What would it be like to be held by him? To be pressed against that muscular physique while his fingertips touched her aching breasts?

Aware that her cheeks had grown flushed, she lifted

her eyes to his, wondering what had happened to all her certainties. 'Is there…is there anything else you need?'

He wondered what she would do if he answered that question honestly, and a wry smile curved the edges of his lips as he noted her sudden rise in colour. Would her lips fall open with shock if he told her that he longed for her to fall to her knees, to take him in her mouth and suck him? Or would she simply comply with the easy efficiency she showed in all other elements of their working relationship? Would she *swallow?* he found himself wondering irreverently.

His desire rocketed, frustrating him with a heavy throbbing at his aching groin. He needed her out of here. Now. Before he did or said something he might later regret.

'Leave me now, Izzy,' he commanded unsteadily. 'Unless you're planning to stay and watch while I shower?'

CHAPTER FOUR

SOMEHOW, Isobel managed to hold onto her composure until she'd closed the bedroom door, and then she rushed back down the creaky staircase to the kitchen. Once there, she leaned against one of the cupboards, her eyes squeezed tight shut as she tried not to think about the Sheikh's powerful body, which would soon be acquainting itself with her ancient little bathroom. Her heart was hammering as an imagination she hadn't known she possessed began to taunt her with vivid images.

She thought about Tariq naked. With little droplets of water gleaming against his flesh.

She thought about Tariq drying—the towel lingering on his damp, golden flesh as he rubbed himself all over.

Swallowing down the sudden lump which had risen in her throat, she shook her head. Weaving erotic fantasies about him would lead to nothing but trouble—and so would baring her soul. Taking Tariq into her confidence would only add to the vulnerability she was already experiencing. She wondered what had made her confide in him about her father, and the fact that she'd never known him.

She knew she had to pull herself together. *She* had

been the one who'd invited him to stay, and he was going to be here for the next few days whether she liked it or not. Just because her feelings towards him seemed to have changed—what mattered was that she didn't let it show.

Because Tariq was no fool. He was a master of experience when it came to the opposite sex, and he was bound to start noticing her reaction if she wasn't careful. If she dissolved into mush every time he came near, or her fingers started trembling just like they were doing now, wouldn't that give the game away? Wouldn't he guess that her senses had been shaken into life and she'd become acutely attracted to him? And just how embarrassing would that be?

She needed a plan. Something to stop him from dominating her mind with arousing thoughts.

Opening the door of the freezer, she peered inside and began to devise a crash course in displacement therapy which would see her through the days ahead. She would make sure she had plenty to occupy her. She would be as brisk and efficient as she was at work, and maybe this crazy *awareness* of him would go away.

But that was easier said than done. By the time Tariq came back downstairs she was busy chopping up ingredients for a risotto, but she made the mistake of lifting her head to look at him. And then found herself mesmerised by the intimate image of her boss fresh from the bath. His hair was damp and ruffled, and he carried with him the faint tang of her ginger and lemon gel.

Isobel swallowed. 'Bath okay?'

He raised his eyebrows. 'You didn't bother telling me that you don't have a shower.'

'I guessed you find out soon enough.'

'So I did,' he growled. 'It's the most ancient bathroom I've used in years—and the water was tepid.'

'Don't they say that tepid baths are healthier?'

'Do they?' He looked around. 'Where's your TV?'

'I don't have one.'

'You don't have a TV?'

Isobel shot him a defensive look. 'It isn't mandatory, you know. There's a whole wall of books over there. Help yourself to one of those.'

'You mean *read?*'

'That *is* what people usually do with books.'

With a short sigh of impatience, Tariq wandered over to examine the neat rows of titles which lined an entire wall of her sitting room.

The only things he ever read were financial papers or contracts, or business-related articles he caught up with when he was travelling. Occasionally his attention would be caught by some glossy car magazine, which would lure him into changing his latest model for something even more powerful. But he never read books. He had neither the time nor the inclination to lose himself in the world of fiction. He remembered that stupid story he'd read at school—about some animal which had been abandoned. He remembered the tears which had welled up in his eyes when its mother had been shot and the way he'd slammed the volume shut. Books made you *feel* things—and the only thing he wanted to feel right now were the tantalising curves of Izzy's body.

But that was a *bad* idea. And he needed something to occupy his thoughts other than musing about what kind of underwear a woman like that would wear beneath her rather frumpy clothes.

In the end he forced himself to read a thriller—grateful for the novel's rapid pace, which somehow seemed to suck him into an entirely believable story of a one-time lap dancer successfully nailing a high-profile banker for fraud. He was so engrossed in the tale that Izzy's voice startled him, and he looked up to find her standing over him, her face all pink and shiny.

'Mmm?' he questioned, thinking how soft and kissable her lips looked.

'Supper's ready.'

'Supper?'

'You *do* eat supper?'

Actually he usually ate *dinner*—an elegant feast of a meal—rather than a large spoonful of glossy rice slapped on the centre of an earthy-looking plate. But to Tariq's surprise he realised that he was hungry—and he enjoyed it more than he had expected. Afterwards Izzy heaped more logs on the fire, and they sat there in companionable silence while he picked up his novel and began to race through it again.

For Tariq, the days which followed his accident were unique. He'd been brought up in a closeted world of palaces and privilege, but now he found himself catapulted into an existence which seemed far more bizarre.

His nights were spent alone, in an old and lumpy bed, yet he found he was sleeping late—something he rarely did, not even when he was jet-lagged. And the lack of a shower meant that he'd lie daydreaming in the bath in the mornings. In the cooling water of the rather cramped tub he would stretch out his long frame and listen to the sounds of birds singing outside the window. So that by the time he wandered downstairs it was to find his Titian-haired assistant bustling around with milk jugs and muesli, or asking him if he wanted to try the eggs from the local farm.

For the first time in a long time he felt *relaxed*—even if Izzy seemed so busy that she never seemed to stop. She was always doing *something*—cooking or cleaning or dealing with the e-mails which flooded in from the office, shielding him from all but the most necessary requests.

'Why don't you loosen up a little?' he questioned one morning, glancing up from his latest thriller to see her cleaning out the grate, a fine cloud of coal dust billowing around her.

Izzy pushed a stray strand of hair from out of her eyes with her elbow. Because action distracted her from obsessing about his general gorgeousness, that was why. And because she was afraid that if she allowed herself to stop then she might never get going again.

What did he expect her to do all day? Sit staring as he sprawled over her sofa, subjecting her to a closer-than-was comfortable view of his muscular body? Watch as he shifted one powerful thigh onto the other, thus drawing attention to the mysterious bulge at the crotch of his jeans? A place she knew she shouldn't be looking—which, of course, made it all the more difficult not to. She felt guilty and ashamed at the wayward path of her thoughts, and began to wonder if he had cast some kind of spell on her. Suddenly the clingy behaviour of some of his ex-lovers became a little more understandable.

Her nights weren't much better. How could they be when she knew that Tariq was lying in bed in the room next door? Hadn't she already experienced the disturbing episode of him wandering out of the bathroom one

morning with nothing but a small towel strung low
around his hips?

Tiny droplets of water had clung to his hard, olive-
skinned torso, and Isobel's heart had thumped like a pis-
ton as she'd surveyed his perfect physique. She'd briefly
thought of suggesting that perhaps he ought to be using
a bigger towel. But wouldn't that have sounded awfully
presumptuous? In the end, she had just mumbled, 'Good
morning...' and hurried past him, terrified that he would
see the telltale flush of desire in her cheeks.

Almost overnight the cool neutrality she'd felt towards her boss had been replaced with new and scary
sensations. She felt almost molten with longing whenever she looked at him—yet at the same time she resented these disturbing new feelings. Why couldn't
she have felt this sharp sense of desire with other men?
Decent, reliable men? The kind of men she usually dated
and who inevitably left her completely cold? Why the
hell did it have to be *him?*

'Izzy?' His deep voice broke into her disturbed
thoughts. 'Why don't you sit down and relax?'

'Oh, I'm happier when I'm working,' she hedged, as
she swept more dust out of the fireplace. 'Anyway, we're
going back to London tomorrow.'

'We are?' He put his book down and frowned. 'Has
it really been a week?'

'Well, five days, actually—but you certainly seem
better.'

'I feel better,' he said, acknowledging that this was
something of an understatement. He hadn't felt like this
in years—as if every one of his senses had been retuned
and polished. He was looking forward to getting back
to London and hitting the ground running.

But his last night in Izzy's little cottage was restless, and the sound sleep he'd previously enjoyed seemed to elude him. Inexplicably, he found himself experiencing a kind of regret that he wouldn't ever sleep in this old-fashioned bed again, beneath the flower-sprigged linen. He lay awake, wondering if he was imagining the sound of Izzy moving in her sleep next door, her slim, pale limbs tossing and turning. Maybe he was—but he certainly wasn't imagining his reaction to those thoughts.

With a small groan he turned onto his side, and then onto his stomach—feeling the rising heat of yet another erection pressing against the mattress. It had been like this for most of the week, and it had been hell. Night after night he'd imagined parting Izzy's pale thighs and sliding his hot, hard heat into her exquisite warmth. He swallowed as the tightness increased. Was his body so starved of physical pleasure that he should become fixated on a woman simply because she happened to be *around?* Yet what other explanation could there be for this inexplicable lust he was experiencing?

In the darkness of the bedroom he heard the distant hoot of an owl in the otherwise silent countryside and his mouth thinned. He needed a lover, that was for sure—and the moment he got back to London he'd do something about it. Maybe contact that beautiful Swedish model who had been coming on to him so strong...

Resisting the urge to satisfy himself, he buried his cheek against a pillow which smelt of lavender, and yawned as he fantasised about a few more likely candidates.

But sleep still eluded him, and at first light he gave up the fight, tugged on a pair of jeans and went downstairs—still yawning. He made strong coffee in Izzy's outdated percolator, and after he'd drunk it settled down to finish his thriller.

And that was where Isobel found him a couple of hours later—stretched out on the sofa, the book open against the gentle rise and fall of his chest. The feathery dark arcs of his lashes did not move when she walked in, and she realised that he was fast asleep.

Her barefooted tread was silent as she padded across the room towards him, unable to resist the temptation to observe him at closer quarters—telling herself that she only wanted to see if he looked rested and recovered. To see whether it really was a good idea for him to go back to London later that day.

But that was a lie and she knew it. Deep down she knew she was going to miss this crazy domestic arrangement. Despite the pressure of wanting him, she had enjoyed sharing her living space with her boss. Even if it had been an artificial intimacy which they'd created between them, it didn't seem to matter. She'd seen another side to him—a more *human* side—and she couldn't help wondering what it would be like once they were back in the office.

Yet, despite her mixed thoughts, she felt a quiet moment of pride as she looked down at him—because he was certainly back to his usual robust self. If anything, he looked better than she could ever remember seeing him. Less strained. More relaxed. His olive skin was highlighted with a glorious golden glow, and his lips were softened at the edges.

But the hard beating of her heart made her realise that her new-found feelings for him hadn't gone away. That stupid softness hadn't hardened into her habitual indifference towards him. Something had changed—or maybe the feeling had always been there, deep down. Maybe it was a left-over crush from her schooldays and she'd only buried it rather than abandoning it. But, either way, she didn't know what she was going to do about it.

She continued to stare at him, willing herself to feel nothing—but to no avail. She was itching to touch him, even in the most innocent of ways. Because what other way did she know? A thick ebony lock of hair had curled onto his forehead, and she had to resist the impulse to smooth it away with the tips of her fingers.

But maybe she moved anyway—if only fractionally—because his lashes suddenly fluttered open to reveal the watchful black gleam of his eyes.

Did she suck in a sudden breath and then expel it with a sigh which shuddered out from somewhere deep in her lungs? The kind of sigh which could easily be mistaken for longing? Was that why his arm suddenly snaked up without warning, effortlessly curling around her waist before bringing her down onto his bare chest in one fluid movement?

'T-Tariq!' she gasped, feeling the delicious impact as their bodies made unexpected contact.

'Izzy,' he growled, as every fantasy he'd been concocting over the last few days burst into rampant life.

Izzy with her hair loose and cascading around her shoulders. Izzy wearing some ridiculously old-fashioned pair of pyjamas. Izzy warm and soft and smelling of toothpaste, just begging to be kissed. Reaching up, he tangled his fingers in the rich spill of her curls and brought her mouth down on his.

'Oh!' Her startled exclamation was muffled by his kiss, and it only partially blotted out the urgent clamour of her thoughts. She ought to stop him. She knew that. A whole lifetime of conditioning told her so.

But Isobel didn't stop him, and the words which her mother had once drummed into her floated straight out of her mind. It no longer mattered that Tariq was the worst possible person to let make love to her. Because her body was on fire—a fire created by the blazing heat of his. She wanted him, and she wanted his kiss. She wanted it enough to turn her back on all her so-called principles, and now she gave in to it with greedy fervour, her mouth opening hungrily beneath his.

She could hear the small moan he made as the kiss deepened. He crushed his lips against hers and a fierce heat began to flood through her body, from breast to belly and beyond.

Frantically, her fingers slithered over his chest and began to knead at the silken flesh, feeling the mad hammer of his heart against her palm. She moaned into his mouth as his hand skimmed down from the base of her throat to her breast, slipping his fingers inside her pyjama jacket and capturing the aching mound with proprietorial skill. She could feel him stroking one pinpoint nipple between finger and thumb until she gasped aloud, wriggling uselessly as she felt the flagrant ridge at his groin pressing against her belly.

Tariq groaned. She tasted of mint, and her hair tickled him as the thick curls cascaded down the side of her face. She felt *amazing*. Was that because this had come at him out of the blue? Or was it novelty value because she was the last person in the world he could imagine responding with such easy passion? My God, she was *hot*.

He kissed her until he had barely any breath left in

his lungs, and it became apparent that her narrow sofa was hopelessly inadequate for two people who were exploring each other's bodies for the first time.

'This is getting a little crowded,' he managed, pulling his lips away from hers with an effort.

He slid them both to the ground, barely noticing the hard flagstones beneath the thin rug. All that concerned him was the gasping beauty in his arms, her hair spilling out all over the floor like tendrils of pale fire and her eyes as tawny as a tiger's.

'Comfortable?' he questioned, as he smoothed some of the wiry corkscrews away from the pink flush of her cheeks.

Heart thundering, Isobel gazed up at him, wondering why she didn't feel shyer than she did. Was it because Tariq was staring down at her with such gleaming hunger in his eyes that in that moment she felt utterly desirable? As if almost *anything* was possible? 'Oddly enough, yes, I am.'

'Me too. Deliciously comfortable. Perhaps I can help make you more comfortable still, *anisah bahiya.*' Pulling open her dressing gown, he began to unbutton her pyjamas—until two rosy-peaked breasts were thrusting towards him. Unable to resist their silent plea, he bent his head to suckle one. Slicking his tongue against the tight bud, he felt the responsive jerk of her hips and heard her gasp his name. 'I've never seduced a woman in pyjamas before,' he whispered against the puckered flesh.

'Are you…are you going to seduce me, then?'

'What do you think? That I've got you down here because I want to discuss my diary for next week?'

Thinking was the last thing Isobel wanted to do—because if she did that then surely she would realise that what they were doing was crazy. Wouldn't thinking remind her that Tariq was a cavalier playboy, and that there was a reason why men like him should be avoided like the plague? Wouldn't it prompt her into doing the only sensible thing—which was to tear herself away from him and rush upstairs to her room, away from temptation?

She felt the graze of his teeth against her nipple and shut her eyes. Far better to feel. To allow these amazing sensations to skate over her skin and fill her with an urgent longing which was fast spiralling out of control.

'Oh!' she breathed, eagerly squirming her hips beneath him and feeling a warm, wild heat building up inside her. And he answered her voiceless plea by slipping his hand inside the elasticated waistband of her pyjamas.

She held her breath as his warm palm navigated its way down her belly, tiptoeing tantalisingly to the fuzz of hair which lay beyond. Still she held her breath as he stroked at the sensitive skin of her inner thigh, and then gasped as his fingertips seared over her moist heat.

'Oh!' she said again.

'You're very wet.'

'A-am I?'

'Mmm…' Tariq's mouth brushed over hers as his finger strayed to the tight bud at the very core of her desire. Her instant compliance didn't surprise him—he was capable of reducing a woman to a boneless state of longing no matter what the circumstances. But the sheer and urgent spontaneity of what they were doing made him tense—just for a moment. And that moment was enough for him to remember one vital omission.

He froze, before snatching his hand away from her. Damn and damn and *damn!*

'I don't have any protection with me,' he ground out.

For one stupid moment Isobel thought he was talking about the bodyguards he sometimes used, and then she saw the look of dark frustration on his face and realised what he meant. A wave of insecurity washed over her.

Should she tell him?

Of *course* she should tell him—they were on the brink of making love, and now was not the time for coyness.

'Actually, I'm...' Isobel swallowed, wanting his fingers back on her aching flesh. 'I'm on the pill.'

Her admission dampened his ardour fractionally. He drew away from her, his black eyes slitted in a cool question. 'The pill?'

Isobel heard the unmistakable disapproval in his voice. 'Lots of women are.'

There was a pause. 'Yes. I imagine that they are.'

Suddenly she shrank from the truth in his hard black eyes, indignant words tumbling from her lips before she could stop them. 'I suppose you think that the kind of woman who happens to have contraception covered is easy?'

Tariq shrugged. 'You must agree that it does imply a certain degree of *accessibility.*'

'Well, you couldn't be more wrong, Tariq,' she declared hotly. 'Because...because I've never had a lover before!'

He stared at her, genuinely confused. 'What the hell are you talking about?'

'I was prescribed the pill because my periods are

heavy, and that's the only reason. I've… Well, I've never had any other reason to take it.'

This commonplace and unexpected disclosure highlighted the unusual degree of intimacy between them, and Tariq frowned. He brushed a corkscrew lock of hair away from her forehead, trying to make sense of her words. 'You're trying to tell me you're—?'

'Yes, I'm a virgin,' she said, as if it didn't matter.

Because surely it didn't? What mattered was Tariq kissing her and transporting her back to that heavenly place he'd taken her to before. Just because she had waited a long time for a man to turn her on as much as this, it didn't mean that she should be treated as some kind of leper, did it?

Sliding her arms around his neck, she lifted her face to his, hungry for him. 'Now, kiss me again,' she whispered.

How could he refuse her soft entreaty? Tariq groaned as he tasted her trembling lips and a shaft of pure desire shot through him. He could feel the softness of her breasts yielding against his bare chest, their taut tips firing at him like little arrows towards his heart. Irresistibly, his fingers slipped inside the waistband of her pyjama trousers again, and he heard her little gurgle of anticipation.

For one moment he was about to peel them right off. Then his hand paused, mid-motion, as he forced himself to recall the unbelievable facts.

She was a virgin!

And more importantly…

She was his assistant!

'No!' he thundered, dragging his lips away from hers. 'I will not do this!'

Her body screaming out its protest, Isobel looked up at him in confusion. 'Will not do what?'

'I will not rob you of your innocence!'

She stared at him, still not understanding. 'Why not?'

'Are you crazy? Because a woman's purity is her greatest gift. And it's a one-off—you don't get to use it again. So save it for a man who will give you more than I ever can, Izzy. Don't throw it away on someone like me.'

For a moment he cupped her chin between his palms, looking down at her with a regret which only compounded her intense feeling of rejection. She jerked her face away—as if to allow him continued contact might in some way contaminate her.

'Then w-would you mind moving away from me and letting me get up?' she said, trembling hurt distorting her words.

'I can try.' With a grimace, he rose to his feet, the heavy throb at his groin making movement both difficult and uncomfortable.

Despite the scene he now rather grimly anticipated he couldn't help a flicker of admiration as he looked at Isobel clambering to her feet, tugging furiously at the jacket of her pyjamas. Passion always changed a woman, he mused, but in Izzy's case it had practically *transformed* her. Her hair was falling in snake-like tendrils all around her slender shoulders and she stood before him like some bright and unrecognisable sorceress. For a moment he experienced a deep sense of regret and frustration—and then he steeled his heart against his foolishness and turned his back on her.

With shaking fingers Isobel began to do up her pyjamas, realising that she had let herself down—and in so

many ways. She had shown Tariq how much she wanted
him and he had pushed her away, leaving her feeling
guilty that she'd been prepared to 'throw away' her virginity on someone like him. How did you ever get back
from something like that? The dull truth washed over
her. The answer was that you didn't.

Biting her lip, she watched as he turned away to
adjust his jeans, trying to ignore the sense of having
missed out on something wonderful. Of having been
on the brink of some amazing discovery. Inevitably she
was now going to lose her job, and she didn't even have
the compensation of having known him as a lover. But
surely it was better to face up to the consequences of
her behaviour than to wait for him to put the knife in?

'You want me to hand my notice in?' she asked quietly.

This was enough to make Tariq turn back and scru-
tinise her, steeling himself against the enduring kiss-
ability of her darkened lips, knowing that if he didn't get
out of there soon he'd go back on everything he'd just
said and thrust deep and hard inside her, tear her precious membrane and leave his mark on her for ever. He
shook his head. 'Actually, that's precisely what I *don't*
want. That's one of the reasons I pulled back. I value
you far too much to want to lose you, Izzy.'

In spite of everything, his words took Isobel aback.
In five years of working for him it was the first time
he'd ever said anything remotely like that. She screwed
her face up, wondering how to react to the unfamiliar
compliment. 'You do?'

'Of course I do—and this week has shown me just
how much. I have a lot to thank you for. You're a hard-
working, loyal member of my staff, and I've come to

rely on you a great deal. And believe me—I'd have a lot of trouble replacing you.'

Isobel kept her face expressionless as something inside her withered and died. 'I see.'

'And just because of this one uncharacteristic lapse...'

She grimaced as his voice tailed off. Now he was making her sound like a docile family dog which had unexpectedly jumped up and bitten the postman.

'I don't see why it should have to change anything,' he continued.

'So you want that we should just forget what has happened and carry on as normal?'

'In theory, yes.' His black eyes bored into her. 'Do you think you can do that?'

It was the patronising tone of the question which swung it. Isobel had been on the verge of telling him that she didn't think there was any going back—or forward—but his arrogant assumption that she might struggle with resuming their professional relationship made her blood boil.

'Oh, I don't think *I'd* have a problem with it,' she answered sweetly. 'How about you?'

Tariq's eyes narrowed as she tossed him the throwaway question. Was she now implying that she was some sort of irresistible little sex-bomb who was going to test his formidable powers of self-control once they were back in the office? He gave a slow smile. He thought she might be forgetting herself.

Once she was back in her usual environment, with her hair scraped back and her rather frumpy clothes in place, there would be no reoccurrence of that inexplicable burst of lust. There would be no flower-sprigged pyjamas and soft curves to send out such sizzling and mixed messages, threatening to make a man lose his head.

'I wouldn't over-estimate your appeal, if I were you,' he said coolly. 'Because that would be a big mistake. I can resist you any time I like.'

CHAPTER FIVE

How could he have been so damned *stupid?*

Tariq stared out of the window at the darkening London skyscape which gave his office its magnificent views. Stars were twinkling in the indigo sky, and in the distance he could see the stately dome of St Paul's cathedral.

He should have been on top of the world.

The doctor had given him the all-clear, his car was in the garage being painstakingly mended, and his acquisition of the Premiership team looked almost certain. Khayarzah oil revenues were at an all-time high, and he had received an unexpected windfall from some media shares he'd scooped up last year. It seemed that everything he turned his hand to in the world of commerce flourished. In short, business was booming.

He turned away from the magnificent view, trying to put his finger on what was wrong. Wondering why this infuriating air of discontentment simply would not leave him—no matter how hard he tried to alleviate it.

He gave a ragged sigh, knowing all too well what lay at the heart of his irritation yet strangely reluctant to acknowledge its source. Its sweet and unexpected source...

Izzy.

His rescuer and tormentor. His calm and efficient assistant, with all her contradictory qualities, who had somehow—against all the odds—managed to capture his imagination.

Had it been pure arrogance which had made him so certain that his lust for her would dissolve the moment they were back in the office? He'd decided that the crash had weakened him in all ways—mentally, physically *and* emotionally. He'd thought that was why he had been so curiously susceptible to a woman he had never found in the least bit attractive. An insanity, yes—but a temporary one.

But he had been wrong.

Since being back at work he'd been unable to stop fantasising about her. Or to stop thinking about those prudish pyjamas which had covered up the red-hot body beneath. His mind kept taking him back to their tangled bodies on the floor of her cottage, reminding him of just how close they'd got. If common sense hadn't forced him to call a halt to what was happening he would have... would have...

But it was more than just frustrated lust which was sending his blood pressure soaring. His desire was compounded by knowing that she was a virgin. That she had never known a man's lovemaking before and she had wanted *him*. Just as he had wanted *her*.

He swallowed. The fact that she worked for him and that it was entirely inappropriate did little to lessen his appetite. On the contrary, the thought of making love to her excited him beyond belief—perhaps because it was his first ever taste of the forbidden. And for a man like Tariq very few things in life were forbidden...

His erotic thoughts were interrupted by the cause of

his frustration as Izzy walked in, bearing a tiny cup of inky coffee which she deposited in front of him with a smile. Not the kind of smile he would have expected, in the circumstances. It was not tinged with longing, nor was it edged with a frustration similar to the one he was experiencing. No, it was a bright and infuriatingly sunny smile—a sort of pre-weekend kind of smile. As if she had forgotten all about those passion-fuelled moments back in her country cottage.

Had she?

'You aren't changing?' she questioned.

Tariq blinked at her, her question arrowing into the confusing swirl of his thoughts. 'Changing?' he growled. 'What's wrong with the way I am?'

Isobel felt her heart hammer in response. Oh, but he was edgy this evening! Even edgier than he'd been all week. Mind you, she'd been feeling similarly jumpy—just determined not to show it. Her pride had been shattered by his rejection, and she was determined to salvage what was left of it by maintaining a cool air of composure. But it was difficult trying to pretend that nothing had happened when your boss had fondled your naked breasts and part of you was longing for him to do it all over again.

She tipped her head to one side and pretended to consider his question. 'How long have you got?'

'Izzy—'

'I meant *changing* in a literal sense,' she clarified, with a quick glance at her watch. 'Aren't you due for a party at the Maraban Embassy at seven? And don't you usually wear something dark and tailored instead of...?' Her bravado suddenly evaporated, her voice tailing off as she was momentarily distracted by his physical presence. *Why* had she allowed her eyes to linger on his physique, when she had determinedly been avoiding it all week?

'Instead of what, Izzy?' he questioned silkily, for he had noticed the sudden. rapid blinking of her eyes.

'Instead of...' She realised that he must have removed his tie at some point during the afternoon, and loosened at least two buttons of his shirt. Because rather more of his chest was on show than usual—and it reminded her of his warm, bare flesh beneath her fingertips on the floor of her cottage.

She could see the lush, dark whorls of hair growing there—which added texture to the olive glow of his skin and invited the eye on an inevitable path downwards...

Keep your mind on the job, she urged herself fiercely. *You're not supposed to be lusting after him—remember?*

'It's...it's a formal event, isn't it?' she finished helplessly.

Tariq felt a brief moment of triumph as he saw her eyes darken. So she was *not* completely immune to him—despite the way she'd been behaving all week. His mouth hardened with grudging respect—for Izzy had shown herself to be made of sterner stuff than he would have thought. Since they'd been back in the office she had treated him with exactly the same blend of roguish yet respectful attitude as she'd done all through their professional relationship. As if his being moments away from penetrating her body had left her completely cold. So was that true? Or was it all some kind of act?

He let his eyes drift over her, wondering if she had decided to showcase the dullest items in her wardrobe. Maybe he'd seen that skirt before—and her pale sweater certainly wasn't new—but she looked dowdier than he could ever remember. Was that deliberate? Or was it because now he knew more about her he was looking at her more closely? Comparing how she looked now to how she'd looked when she had been writhing around beneath him? And he couldn't rid himself of the unsettling knowledge of the magnificent rose-tipped and creamy breasts which lay beneath her insipid armour.

'Yes, it's a formal event,' he drawled. 'And, to be truthful, I don't feel like going.'

'But you have to go, Tariq.'

'Have to?' He raised his brows. 'Is that an order?'

'No, of course it isn't.'

He began to walk towards her, noticing the tip of her tongue as it snaked out to moisten her lips 'Why do I have to?' he queried softly.

'Well, your two countries are neighbours, and you've just signed that big trade agreement, and it will look very b-bad if…if…'

He heard her stumbled words with a triumphant kick of pleasure. 'If what?'

Isobel swallowed. What was going on? What was he doing? The gap between them was closing, and instinct made her step backwards—away from his inexorable path towards her. But there was no escaping him despite the massive dimensions of his office. Nowhere to go until she reached a wall and felt its smooth, cool surface at her back. She stared up at him with widened eyes. Wasn't he breaking the agreement they'd made?

'T-Tariq! What do you think you're doing?'

Pushing one hand against the wall right beside her head, he leaned forward and looked deep into her tawny eyes. 'I'm wondering why you're trying to give me lessons in protocol I neither want nor need. But mostly I'm wondering whether you're feeling as frustrated as I am.'

Perhaps if he'd put it any other way than that Isobel might have given his question some consideration—or allowed her feelings to sway her. Because hadn't she been teetering on a knife-edge of wanting him and yet terrified of letting him know that? Hadn't it been as much as she could do each morning not to gaze wistfully at the sensual curve of his cynical lips? Not to wish that they were subjecting her to another of those hard and passionate kisses?

But his question had been more mechanical than emotional. No woman wanted to feel like an itch which a man needed to scratch, did she? And hadn't she told herself over and over again that no matter how much she wanted him no good would come of any kind of liaison? She *knew* about his track record with women. And only someone who was completely insane would lay herself open to an inevitable hurt like that.

'We aren't supposed to be discussing this,' she said flatly.

'Aren't we? Says who?'

'Said *you!* And me! That's what we agreed on back at the cottage. We agreed that it was a mistake. We're supposed to be carrying on as normal and forgetting it ever happened.'

'Maybe we are. But the trouble is...' And now he leaned in a little further towards her, so that he could feel the warm fan of her rapid breathing. 'The trouble is that I'm finding it difficult to forget it ever happened. In fact, it's proving impossible. I keep thinking about how it felt to have you in my arms. About how wild your hair looks when you let it down. I keep remembering what it was like to kiss you, and how your breasts felt when I was touching them.'

'Tariq,' she whispered, as his words made her body spring into instant life and her mouth dried as she stared into his darkening eyes. 'You were the one who stopped it. Remember?'

'And I did that because you're a virgin!' he said, letting his hand fall by his side. 'I decided I had no right to take your innocence from you. That you deserved a man who would cherish you more than I could ever do.'

'Well, that much hasn't changed. I haven't rushed out and leapt into bed with someone else in the meantime. I'm still a virgin, Tariq.'

'I realise that.' Their gazes clashed as he fought to do the decent thing. 'And I still don't think it's the right thing to do.'

She bit her lip. Was he playing games with her? 'So why are we even *having* this conversation?'

For a moment he clenched his fists savagely by his thighs, telling himself that he had no right to take an innocence which would be better given to another man. A man who would love her and cherish her. Who was capable of giving her the things that every woman wanted.

But the soft, sweet tremble of her lips defeated his best intentions, and a ragged sigh shuddered from between his lips. 'Because I'm finding resisting you harder than I anticipated.'

She stared into the heated gleam of his black eyes as a blend of frustration and emotion began to bubble up inside her and that sweet, terrible aching started all over again. 'And what about what *I* think?' she questioned quietly. 'What if I'm finding resisting *you* harder than I thought?'

Once again he fought with his conscience, but this time it was even more difficult because he realised that Izzy was enchantingly unique. An innocent who was up-front about her needs. A woman who wasn't playing coy games. The fists at his sides relaxed, and he lifted his hand and began to trace a light line around the butterfly tremble of her lips.

'You know I can't offer you anything in the way of commitment? That nothing long-term is going to come out of this? Three weeks is about my limit with any woman—you know that better than anyone, Izzy.'

She heard the stark warning in his words, but she wanted him too much to pay them any attention. And she was wise enough not to question him about why he was so adamant about short-term relationships. Maybe she'd ask him another time…just not now. Now she was fighting for something she wasn't prepared to give up on.

'You think that all virgins expect marriage from the first man they sleep with? Er, hello—and welcome to the twenty-first century! Aren't I allowed to do something just because I want to—the way you always seem to do? Just for the hell of it?'

Tariq felt his resistance trickling away. Nobody could say he hadn't tried—but it seemed that Izzy was intent on fighting him every inch of the way. Maybe this *was* the only solution to the otherwise unendurable prospect of the two of them dancing around each other every day, aching with frustrated need. And wasn't there something about making love to her which appealed to him on a very fundamental level? Something which he had never done with any other woman…

'For the hell of it? I think you're selling yourself short.

Why don't we try a taste of heaven instead?' he said, and he pulled her into his arms and let his mouth make a slow motion journey to meet hers.

She actually cried out with pleasure out as he began to kiss her, the taste and feel of his mouth seeming gloriously familiar. Gripping his shoulders, she dug her fingers into his suit jacket, afraid that her knees might give way if she didn't have something to cling onto. And as the kiss grew deeper she could feel the hard jut of his hips, which framed the unmistakable evidence of his arousal. Recklessly she pressed her body closer still, making no protest when he began to ruck her skirt up, urging him on with a guttural little sound of hunger which didn't sound a bit like her.

'Damn tights,' he ground out as his fingers met the least erotic piece of clothing ever designed by man. But he could feel the heat searing through them at the apex of her thighs, and the restless circling of her hips as he touched her there.

With practised ease he yanked them down, slithering them over her knees to her ankles. He knelt to slide off first one shoe and then the other—tossing them aside with the tights, so that they lay discarded. And then he rose again to take her in his arms.

Maybe he should have carried her across to one of the plush sofas which comprised the more casual meeting area of his office. Stripped her off slowly and provocatively as she doubtlessly deserved. But for the first time in his life Tariq couldn't bear the thought of delaying this for a second longer than was necessary. Her wide eyes and quickened breath were doing something inexplicable to him. He felt unaccountably *primitive*...

as if his desire to possess her was urging him along on a dark and unstoppable tide.

He touched her against her panties, heard her make some yelping little sound of pleasure and frustration as he ripped them apart. Then he unzipped himself with a shaking hand, freeing the leaden spring of his erection with a ragged sigh of relief.

She was wet and ready for him, clinging to him eagerly as he thrust into her—hard and deep and without warning. Yet it still came as a shock as he encountered a momentary resistance, and he stilled as he heard her make a little moan of discomfort.

'Aludra!' he choked out, stopping inside her to give her the chance to acclimatise herself to these new sensations. Holding her close, he bent his lips to her ear. 'Did I hurt you, little Izzy?'

She shook her head. 'If you did, then I've forgotten. Please don't stop,' she whispered back, giving a little yelp of pleasure as he began to move inside her. 'It feels...' She closed her eyes and expelled a shuddering breath. 'Oh, Tariq, it feels...*incredible.*'

It felt pretty incredible for him, too. Especially when she wrapped her legs around his back with athletic skill. But it was more than that. He'd never done it like this before. Had never felt this free. This *powerful.* Was that because it was Izzy? A woman who knew him better than any other woman? Didn't that add an extra piquant layer of desire? Or was it because there was no infernal covering of thin rubber between them? He could feel the soft squash of her buttocks as he cupped them, and the deep molten tightness of her body as it welcomed him. He could hear her soft exclamations of pleasure and astonishment, and that too reminded him of the reality.

She's never done this with anyone else.

That possessive thought only sharpened his hunger, and he shuddered with pleasure as he drove deeper and deeper inside her. He spoke to her in half-forgotten words of Khayarzahian as they moved in ancient rhythm, until he heard her make a helpless little cry and felt her begin to convulse around him.

She gasped his name and clutched at his shoulders like a woman who was drowning, and then at last he let go. And it was like nothing he'd ever experienced. One sweet and erotic spasm after another racked through him, until he felt as if he'd been wrung out and left to dry. Her head fell against his shoulder and he could feel the quiver of her unsteady breath as she panted against his neck. Her legs slipped down from his waist and he wrapped his arms around hers and held her very close.

He didn't know how long they stayed like that—just that it seemed like warm and satiated bliss. As if they were in their own private and very erotic bubble. Until he felt himself begin to harden again inside her and knew that he had to move.

Reluctantly he withdrew from her, tilting her face upwards with his hand. Her cheeks were flushed, and some of the Titian corkscrew curls had come loose and were falling untidily around her shoulders. She looked as wanton as any woman could—and light-years away from the woman who had placed a cup of coffee in front of him not long ago.

He felt...*dazed.* And for the first time in his life slightly *bewildered.* That had been *incredible.* And yet slightly perturbing too, for he could never remember being so out of control before.

Pushing away any remaining doubts, he brushed a

dancing corkscrew strand away from her lips, recognising that a latent sense of guilt would serve no useful purpose. 'Well, I don't remember *that* being in your job description,' he murmured.

Isobel took her lead from him. She was obviously supposed to keep it light. Her lips curved into a coquettish smile she'd never used before. 'And did I perform the task to your satisfaction...*sir?*'

Softly, he laughed. 'Well, there'll need to be a repeat session, of course. I can't possibly judge after just one performance.'

Performance? The word cut through her heightened senses and Isobel bit her lip, suddenly feeling way out of her depth. 'And was I...?'

'You were amazing,' he reassured her softly. 'In fact you were more than amazing.'

He stared down into her face as if he was seeing it for the first time—though this was the face that greeted him each day. This was Izzy—who told him the truth when he asked her. And sometimes when he didn't ask her. Would sex destroy some of the unique rapport which existed between them? he wondered, as even more questions began to flood into his mind.

'Let's go and sit down,' he said abruptly.

Tugging her skirt back over her naked hips, he led her over to one of the low sofas on the far side of the office. Gently, he pushed her down on it, then slid next to her, his black eyes narrowed and questioning.

'So why?' he queried softly.

She guessed she could have pretended to misunderstand him, but she knew exactly what he meant. And that was the trouble—she knew Tariq far too well to play games with him. 'Why am I a virgin, you mean?'

'Wrong tense,' he corrected acidly.

Slightly flustered, she looked at him, seeking refuge in flippancy. 'Because you make me work such long hours that I hardly ever have the opportunity to meet any other men?'

'Izzy. I'm serious. Why?'

She sighed. 'Because… Oh, Tariq. Why do you think?'

Because no man had ever come close to the way he'd made her feel. Because it had been impossible *not* to let him make love to her once they'd started down that path. He'd warned her that there was going to be no long-term or commitment, and she wasn't holding out for any. But that didn't mean she couldn't be honest, did it? Just as long as she kept it cool.

'Because nobody has ever turned me on as much as you do.'

He found himself slightly shocked to hear her talking to him in that way—but that was what he wanted, wasn't it? The fact that she could see their lovemaking for what it was and not construct some romantic fantasy about it the way that women always did?

'It was like that for me too,' he admitted softly. 'In fact…' Hot and erotic memories flooded back. Of skin on skin as she welcomed him into her hot, slick body. He swallowed, acknowledging the potency of what had happened between them. And because of her innocence he felt he owed her the truth. 'It was the best sex of my life.'

Isobel drew away from him, hating the sudden leap of her heart, angry with herself for wanting to buy into what was clearly a lie. And angry with him for feeling that she needed to be placated with a lie as whopping as that one. 'Oh, come on, Tariq—with all the lovers you've had, you're honestly expecting me to believe that?'

'But it is true.' He stared into her now smoky tawny eyes, wondering how much of the truth she could bear. 'You see, never before have I made love to a woman without protection. It is a risk that I can never take— for all the obvious reasons. But a virgin who has never known another man cannot be tainted.' He took her fingers and drifted them over his groin, enjoying seeing her eyes widen as he hardened instantly beneath them. 'And a virgin who is on the pill cannot give me an unwanted child.'

Isobel snatched her hand away. 'So you really hit the jackpot with me?'

He gave a low laugh as he recaptured her hand and brought it up to his lips. 'You wanted to know why I found sex with you more exciting than with anyone else and I've told you. Don't ask the questions, Izzy, if you can't bear to hear the answers.'

'You're impossible,' she whispered.

'And you're...' His eyes narrowed as he kissed each fingertip in turn. 'Well, right now you are looking positively *decadent*.'

Her indignation melted away as he slid her fingers inside the moist cavern of his mouth. It was as if even his most innocuous touch could weaken all her defences. 'Am I?'

'Extremely.' He drifted the now damp fingers to the faint indigo shadows beneath her sleepy tawny eyes. 'But you also look worn out, *kalila.*'

She loved him touching her like that. She loved him touching her pretty much anywhere. 'Mmm?'

'Mmm. So why don't you just relax?' He brushed

back the heavy spill of curls which had fallen down around her face. 'Go on, Izzy. Relax.'

With a little sigh, she let her head drift back against the sofa as he continued to stroke her hair, just as if she were some cat that he was petting.

Distantly, as her weighted eyelids whispered to a close, she could hear the sound of water splashing. For one crazy moment she could have sworn that she heard someone *whistling*. But then the emotion of what had just happened and the stupefying endorphins it had produced made Isobel drift off into a glorious half-world of sleep.

She was woken by the distinct smell of sandalwood and the lightest brush of lips over hers, and when she blinked her eyes open it was to see Tariq standing over her. His black hair was glittering with tiny droplets of water and he was wearing a stark and beautifully cut tuxedo. He must have showered and changed in his office's luxury bathroom, she thought dazedly.

The crisp whiteness of his silk shirt contrasted against the glow of his olive skin, and his black eyes positively *gleamed* with energy and satisfaction. He looked like a perfect specimen of masculinity, she thought—all pumped up and raring to go. As if, for him, sex had been nothing but a very gratifying form of exercise.

She stared up at him. 'What's...what's happening?'

Tariq swallowed down a surge of lust. She looked so damned sexy lying there that part of him wanted to carry on where they'd left off. To do it to her again—only more slowly this time, and on the comfort of a couch. But wouldn't some kind of natural break be better—for both of them? Wouldn't that allow them to put some necessary perspective on what had just happened—and

allow her not to start reading too much into what could
be a potentially awkward situation?

'You know I have to go to the party at the Maraban
Embassy,' he said softly. 'You were nagging me about
it before we…'

Isobel kept the stupefied smile glued to her lips. *He
was still planning on going to the party!*

'Yes. Yes, of course. You must go.' She struggled
to sit up a little, but Tariq made matters even worse
by leaning over her and stroking a strand of hair away
from her lips with the tip of his thumb. For a moment
his thumb lingered, tracing its way around the sudden
tremble of her lips.

'I'll get my car to drop you off home,' he said.

'No, honestly. I can get the—'

'Bus?'

'Well, yes.'

'Without your panties?' His rueful gaze drifted across
the room to where her ripped knickers were lying in a
crumpled little heap of silk. 'I don't think so, *anisah.*
So go and quickly run a brush through your hair, and
then we'll go.'

It was rather a grim end to an eventful afternoon, and
one which made Isobel question the wisdom of what she
had just done. Quickly she availed herself of his bathroom, dragging the Titian curls into some sort of order
and straightening her clothes before they went down in
the elevator to his waiting car.

There was no back seat kiss, no telling her that she
was the most gorgeous woman he'd ever met and that
he would spend the evening thinking about her. Instead
all proprieties were observed as Tariq spent the short

journey to the Maraban Embassy tapping on the flat, shiny screen of his laptop.

When the car pulled up and he looked up he seemed almost to have forgotten who he was with.

'Izzy,' he said softly.

She looked at him, aware that he looked impeccably groomed in comparison to the rumpled exterior she must be presenting. Was he regretting what had happened? Wondering how he could have allowed himself to get so carried away in the heat of the moment? Well, she didn't know how these things usually worked, but she was determined that he should have a let-out clause if he wanted one.

Batting him a quick smile, she pointed to the car door, which was already being opened for him. Let him see that she was perfectly cool about what had happened.

'Better hurry along, Tariq,' she said quickly. 'Leave it much later and you'll have missed all the canapés.'

CHAPTER SIX

'I just wanted to check that you got home okay. The party at the Embassy went on longer than I thought. In fact it was a bit of a bore. I should have stayed right where I was and carried on with exactly what I was doing.' There was a pause before the distinctive voice deepened. *'I'll see you in the office tomorrow, Izzy.'*

With an angry jab of her finger Isobel erased the message on the answer-machine and made her way out to her tiny kitchen; where the morning sunshine was streaming in. It was a strangely unsatisfying message from the man she'd given her virginity to—Tariq must have left it late last night, after she'd gone to bed. But what had she expected? Softness and affection? Tender words as an after-sex gesture? Why would he bother with any of that when she'd practically *begged* him to have sex with her?

She stared at the piece of bread which had just popped out of the toaster and then threw it straight into the bin. She wasn't in the mood for breakfast. She wasn't in the mood for anything, come to think of it, except maybe crawling right back under the duvet and staying there for the rest of the week. She certainly wasn't up for going into work this morning to face her boss after what had happened in the office last night.

She closed her eyes as a shiver raced over her skin, scarcely able to believe what she'd done. Taken complete leave of her senses by letting Tariq have wild sex with her, pressed up against the wall of his office. After years spent wondering if maybe she didn't *have* the sexual impulses of most normal women, of wondering if her mother had poisoned her completely against men, she had discovered that she was very normal indeed.

Behind her eyelids danced tormenting memories. Was that why she'd behaved as she had? Because a lifetime of longing had hit her in a single tidal wave? Or was it simply because it was Tariq and subconsciously she'd wanted him all along?

She shuddered. She'd been like a woman possessed— urging him on as if she couldn't get enough of him. It had been the very first time she'd ever let a man make love to her, and she'd been so greedy for him that she hadn't wanted to wait. She felt the dull flush of shame as she acknowledged that she hadn't even been ladylike enough to hold out for doing it in private—in a *bed!*

Yet she *knew* what kind of man he was. Hadn't she seen him in action often enough in the past? She'd lost count of the times she'd been dispatched to buy last-minute presents for his current squeeze—or bouquets of flowers when he was giving chase to a new woman.

And what about when he started to cool towards the object of his affections, so that he became positively arctic overnight, usually three to four weeks into the 'relationship'? She'd witnessed the faint frown and the shake of his head when she mouthed the name of some poor female whose voice was stuttering down the telephone line as she asked to speak to him. She'd even seen him completely cold-shoulder one hysterical blonde who'd been lying in wait for him outside the Al Hakam building. Then had had his security people bundle her into a car and drive her away at speed. Isobel remembered watching the woman's beautiful features contorted with rage as she glared out of the back window of the limousine.

Time and time again she had told herself that any woman who went to bed with Tariq needed her head examined—and now she had done exactly that. Was she really planning to join the long line of women who had been intimate with him and then had their hearts broken into smithereens?

She stared at her grim-faced reflection in the mirror.

No, she was not.

She was going to have to be grown-up about the whole thing. Men and women often made passionate mistakes—but *intelligent* men and women could soon forget about them. She would go in to work this morning and she would show him—and herself—how strong she could be. She would surprise him with her maturity and her ability to pretend that nothing had happened.

So she resisted the urge to wear a new blouse to work, putting on instead a fine wool dress in a soft heathery colour and tying her hair back as she always did.

Outside it was a glorious day, and the bus journey into work should have been uplifting. The pale blue sky and the fluffy clouds, the unmistakable expectancy of springtime, had lightened people's moods. The bus-driver bade her a cheerful good morning, and the security man standing outside the Al Hakam building was uncharacteristically friendly.

The first part of the day went better than she'd expected—but that was mainly because Tariq was away from the office, visiting the Greenhill Polo Club in Sussex, which he'd bought from the Zaffirinthos royal family last year.

She juggled his diary, answered a backlog of e-mails, and dealt with a particularly persistent sports journalist.

It was four o'clock by the time he arrived back, and Isobel was so deep in work in the outer office that for a moment she didn't hear the door as it clicked open.

It was only when she lifted her head that she found herself caught in the ebony crossfire of his gaze. His dark hair was ruffled, and he had the faint glow which followed hard physical exercise. He looked so arrogantly alpha and completely sexy in that moment that her heart did a little somersault in her chest, despite all her best intentions. She wondered if he'd been riding one of his own polo ponies while he'd been down at Greenhill, and her imagination veered off the strict course she'd proscribed for it. She'd seen him play polo before, and for a moment she imagined him astride one of his ponies, his powerful thighs gripping the flanks of the magnificent glistening animal...

Stop it, she told herself, as she curved her lips into what she hoped was her normal smile. No fantasising—and definitely no flirting. It's business as usual. It might be difficult to begin with, but he's bound to applaud your professionalism in the end.

'Hello, Tariq,' she said, her fingers stilling on the keyboard. 'Good day at Greenhill? I've had the *Daily Post* on the phone all morning. They want to know if it's true that you've been making approaches to buy a defender from Barcelona. I think they were trying to trick me into revealing whether the football club deal is still going ahead. I told him no comment.'

Tariq dropped his briefcase to the floor and frowned. He'd been anticipating...

What?

A blush *at the very least!* Some stumbled words which would acknowledge the amazing thing which had taken place last night. Maybe even a little pout of her unpainted lips to remind him of how good it had felt to kiss them. But not that cool and non-committal look which she was currently directing at him.

'I'll make you a coffee,' she said, rising to her feet.

'I don't want coffee.'

'Tea?'

'I don't want tea either,' he growled. 'Come over here.'

'Where?'

'Don't be disingenuous, Izzy. I want to kiss you.'

Desperately she shook her head, telling herself that she couldn't risk a repeat of what had happened. He was *dangerous.* She *knew* that. If she wasn't careful he would break her heart—just as he'd broken so many others in the past. And the closer she let him get the greater the danger. 'I don't want to kiss you.'

He walked across the office towards her, a sardonic smile curving his lips as he reached for her, his hand snaking around her waist as he pulled her close. 'Well, we both know that's a lie,' he drawled, and he brushed his lips over hers.

Isobel swayed, and for a moment she succumbed— the way women sometimes succumbed to chocolate at the end of a particularly rigid diet. Her lips opened beneath his kiss, and for a few brief seconds she felt herself being sucked into a dark and erotic vortex as he pressed his hard body into hers. Her limbs became boneless as she felt one powerful thigh levering its way between hers, so that she gave an instinctive little wriggle of her hips against it.

Until common sense sounded a warning bell in her head.

Quickly she broke the contact and stepped away from him, her cheeks flushing. She cooled them with the tips of her trembling fingers. 'D-don't.'

'Don't?' he echoed incredulously. 'Why not?'

His arrogant disbelief only made her more determined. 'Isn't it obvious?'

'Not to me.'

'Because...because I don't want to. How's that for clarification?'

Tariq's gaze ran over her darkened eyes and the tell-tale thrust of the taut nipples which were tightening against her dress. His lips curved into a mocking line as he transferred his gaze to her face. 'Really?' he questioned softly. 'I think the lady needs to get honest with herself.'

Stung by the slur, but also aware of the contradictions in her behaviour, Isobel shook her head. 'Oh, Tariq— please don't look at me like that. I'm not saying that I'm not attracted to you—'

'Well, thank heavens for that.' He gave a short laugh. 'For a moment I thought my technique might be slipping.'

'I don't think there's any danger of that,' she said drily. 'But I've been thinking about last night—'

'Me, too. In fact I have thought of little else.' His voice softened, but the blaze in his black eyes was searing. 'You're now regretting the loss of your innocence? Perhaps blaming me for what happened?'

She shook her head. 'No, of course I'm not blaming you. I'm not blaming anyone,' she said carefully. 'It's just I feel I'm worth more than a quick fumble in the office—'

'A *fumble?*' he interrupted furiously. 'This is how you dare to describe what happened between us?'

'How would *you* describe it, then?'

'With a little more poetry and imagination than that!'

'Okay. That...that amazing sex we had, pressed up against the wall of your office.' She sucked in a deep breath—because if she didn't tell him what was bugging her then how would he know? 'And you then treating me like a total stranger in the car before waltzing off to your fancy party at the embassy.'

Tariq narrowed his eyes with sudden comprehension. So *that* was what this was about. She wanted what all women wanted. Recognition. A place on his arm to illustrate their closeness—to show the world their togetherness. But wasn't she being a little *presumptuous,* in the circumstances?

'I didn't touch you because I knew what would happen if I did—and I had no intention of walking into the party with the smell of your sex still on my skin. No.' He shook his head as he saw her open her mouth to speak. 'Let me finish, Izzy. It would have been inappropriate for me to take you to the party,' he added coolly. 'For a start, you weren't exactly dressed for it.'

'You mean I would have let you down?'

'I think you would have felt awkward if you'd gone to a party in your rumpled work clothes, post-sex. Especially to a diplomatic function like that.'

'I'm surprised you know the meaning of the word *diplomatic,*' she raged, 'when you can come out with a statement as insulting as that!'

'I was trying to be honest with you, Izzy,' he said softly. 'Isn't that what this is all about?'

His question took the wind right out of her sails. She supposed it was. She had no right to be angry with him just because he wasn't telling her what she wanted to hear. If he'd come out with some flowery, untrue reason why he hadn't taken her to the embassy, wouldn't she have called him a hypocrite?

'Maybe last night should never have happened,' she said in a small voice.

Ignoring the sudden hardening of his body, Tariq thought about the mercurial nature of her behaviour. Last night she had been *wild* and today she was like ice. Was she testing him to see how far she could push him? She had turned away from him now, so that he got a complete view of her thick curls tied back in a ribbon and a dress he'd seen many times before. Nobody could accuse Izzy of responding to their lovemaking by becoming a vamp in the office. She was probably the least glamorous woman he'd ever met.

Yet the strange thing was that he wanted her. Actually, he wanted her more than he had done yesterday. The contrast between her rather unremarkable exterior and the red-hot lover underneath had scorched through his defences. The memory of how she had yielded so eagerly wouldn't leave him. But it was more than a purely visceral response. Her freshness and eagerness had been like sweet balm applied to his jaded senses. Hadn't she given him more than any

other woman had ever done—surrendering her innocence with such eagerness and joy?

And yet what had he done for her? Taken that innocence in as swift a way as possible and offered her nothing in return. Not even dinner. He felt the unfamiliar
stab of guilt.

'What are you doing tonight?' he said.

The question made Isobel turn round. 'It's my book
club.'

'Your book club?'

'Six to eight women,' she explained, since he'd clearly
never heard of the concept. 'We all read a book and then
afterwards we sit round and discuss it.'

He knitted his brows together. 'And that's supposed
to be enjoyable?'

'That's the general idea.'

'Cancel it.' The answering smile he floated her was
supremely confident. 'Have dinner with me instead.'

Shamefully, she was almost tempted to do as he
suggested—until she imagined the reaction of her girlfriends. Hadn't she let them down enough times in the
past, when Tariq had been in the middle of some big
deal and she'd had to work right through the night? Did
he really expect her to drop everything now, just so he
could get a duty dinner out of the way before another
bout of sex?

She thought about everything she'd vowed. About not
leaving herself vulnerable to heartbreak—which wasn't
going to be easy now that she *had* taken such a big leap
in that direction. But even if she had made herself vulnerable she didn't have to compound it by being a total
doormat.

'I don't want to cancel it, Tariq—I'm hosting in my

apartment. There's two bottles of white wine chilling in the fridge and we're reading *Jane Eyre.*'

Damn *Jane Eyre,* he thought irreverently—but something about her resistance made his lips curve into a sardonic smile.

'What about tomorrow night, then? Do you think you might be able to find a space in your busy schedule and have dinner with me then?' he questioned sarcastically.

Her heart began thundering as she stared at him. Wasn't that what she'd wanted all along? The cloak of respectability covering up the fact that they'd had sex without any of the usual preliminaries? Wouldn't a civilised meal prevent their relationship from being defined by that one rather steamy episode—no matter what happened in the future? Because the chances were that they might decide never to have sex again. Maybe in a restaurant, with the natural barrier of a table between them and the attentions of the waiting staff, they could agree that, yes, it had been a highly pleasurable experience—but best kept as a one-off.

Isobel nodded. 'Yes, I can have dinner with you tomorrow night.'

'Good. Book somewhere, will you? Anywhere you like.'

His expression was thoughtful as he walked through to his inner sanctum. Because this was a first on many levels, he realised.

The first time he'd ever had sex with a member of his staff.

And the first time a woman had ever turned him down for a dinner date.

CHAPTER SEVEN

'This is the last kind of place I'd have thought you'd choose,' said Tariq slowly.

Isobel looked up from the laminated menu, which she already knew by heart, and stared at the hawk-like beauty of the Sheikh's autocratic features. 'You don't like it?'

He looked around. It was noisy, warm and cluttered. Lighted candles dripped wax down the sides of old Chianti bottles, posters of Venice and Florence vied for wall-space with photos of Siena's football team, and popular opera played softly in the background. He could remember eating somewhere like this years ago as a student, at the end of a rowdy rugby tour. But never since then. 'It's…different,' he observed. 'Not the kind of place I normally eat in. I thought you might have chosen somewhere…'

'Yes?' Isobel raised her eyebrows.

'Somewhere a little more upmarket. The kind of place you'd always wanted to go but never had the chance.'

Isobel put the menu down. 'You mean somewhere like the Green Room at the Granchester? Or the River Terrace? Or one of those other fancy establishments with a celebrity chef, where you can only ever get a table at short notice if you happen to *be* someone? All the places *you* usually frequent?'

'They happen to be very good restaurants.'

She leaned forward. '*This* happens to be a good restaurant, too—though you seem to be judging it without even trying it. Just because you don't have to take out a mortgage to eat here, it doesn't mean the food isn't delicious. Actually, I thought *you* might like to try somewhere different and a bit more relaxing. Somewhere you aren't known, since you often complain about rubbernecking people staring at you.' She sat back in her chair again and shot him a challenge with her eyes. 'But maybe you like being looked at more than you care to admit—and anonymity secretly freaks you out?'

He gave a soft laugh. 'Actually, I'm rather enjoying the anonymity,' he murmured, and glanced down at the menu. 'What do you recommend?'

'Well, they make all their own pasta here.'

'And it's good?'

'It's more than good. It's *to die for.*'

His gaze drifted up to the curve of her breasts, which were pert and springy and outlined by a surprisingly chic little black dress. 'I thought women didn't eat carbs.'

'Maybe the sorts of women you know don't,' she said, thinking about his penchant for whip-thin supermodels and feeling a sudden stab of insecurity. 'Personally, I hate all those dietary restrictions. All they do is make people obsessed with eating, or not eating, and their whole lives become about denying themselves what they really want.'

Tariq let that go, realising that he was denying himself what *he* really wanted right at that moment. If it was anyone other than Izzy he would have thrown a large wad of notes down on the tablecloth and told the waiter that they'd lost their appetite. Then taken her back to his apartment and ravished her in every which way he could—before sending out for food.

He realised that he was letting her call the shots, and briefly he wondered why. Because he'd taken her innocence and felt that he owed her? Or was it because she worked for him and his relationship with her was about as equal as any he was likely to have?

'Perhaps we'll have a little role-reversal tonight. How about you choose for me?' he suggested.

'I'd love to.' She beamed.

She lifted her head and instantly the waiter appeared at their table, bearing complementary olives and bread and making a big fuss of her. For possibly the first time in his life Tariq found himself ignored—other than being assured that he was a very lucky man to be eating with such a beautiful woman.

As he leant back in his chair he conceded that the waiter had a point and Izzy *did* look pretty spectacular tonight. For a start she'd let down her hair, so that corkscrew curls tumbled in a fiery cascade around her shoulders. Her silky black dress was far more formal than anything she'd ever worn to work, and it showcased her luscious curves to perfection. A silver teardrop which gleamed at the end of a fine chain hung provocatively between her breasts. And, of course, she had that indefinable glow of sexual awakening…

With an effort, he dragged his gaze away from her cleavage and looked into tawny eyes which had been highlighted with long sweeps of mascara, so that they seemed to dominate her face. 'I take it from the way the waiter greeted you like a long-lost relative that you've been here before?'

'Loads of times. I've been coming here since I first started working in London. It's always so warm and friendly. And at the beginning—when I didn't have much money—they never seemed to mind me spending hours lingering over one dish.'

'Why would they? Restaurants never object to a pretty girl adorning their space. It's a form of free advertising.'

Isobel shook her head. 'Were you born cynical, Tariq?'

'What's cynical about that? It happens to be true. I'm a businessman, Izzy—I analyse marketing opportunities.'

She waited while the waiter poured out two glasses of fizzy water. 'And did you always mean to become a businessman?'

'As opposed to what? A trapeze artist?'

'As opposed to doing something in your own country. Doing something in Khayarzah. You used…'

He frowned as her words trailed off. 'Used to what?'

'At school.' She shrugged as she remembered how sweet he had been to her that time—how he'd made her feel special. A bit like the way he was treating her tonight. 'Well, I hardly knew you at school, of course, but I do remember that one time when you talked about your homeland. You spoke of it in a dreamy way—as if you were talking about some kind of Utopia. And I suppose I sort of imagined…'

'What did you imagine?' he prompted softly.

'Oh, I don't know. That you'd go back there one day.

And live in a palace and fish in that silvery river you described.'

'Ah, but my brother is King there now,' he said, his voice hardening as he acknowledged the capricious law of succession and how it altered the lives of those who were affected by it. 'And Zahid became King very unexpectedly, which changed my place in the natural order of things.'

Isobel looked at him. 'How come?'

'Up until that moment I was just another desert sheikh with the freedom to do pretty much as I wanted—but when our uncle died suddenly I became second in line to the throne. The spare.'

'And is that so bad?' she prompted gently.

'Try living in a goldfish bowl and see how *you* like it,' he said. 'It means you have all the strictures of being the heir, but none of the power. My freedom was something I cherished above everything else...' Hadn't it been the one compensation for his lonely and isolated childhood? The fact that he hadn't really had to account for himself? 'And suddenly it was taken away from me. It made me want to stay away from Khayarzah, where I felt the people were watching me all the time. And I knew that I needed to give Zahid space to settle into his Kingship in peace.' There was a pause. 'Because there is only ever room for one ruler.'

'And do you miss it? Khayarzah, I mean?'

He studied her wide tawny eyes, realising that he had told her more than he had ever told anyone. In truth, his self-imposed exile had only emphasised his feelings of displacement, of not actually belonging anywhere. Just like the little boy who had been sent away to school. As a child he'd felt as if he'd had no real home and as an adult that feeling had not changed.

'Not really,' he mused. 'I go back there on high days and holidays and that's enough. There's no place for me there.'

Isobel sipped her drink as the waiter placed two plates of steaming pasta before them. His last words disturbed her. *There's no place for me there.* Wasn't that an awfully *lonely* thing to say? And wasn't that what she'd thought when she'd seen him lying injured in hospital— that he'd looked so alone? What if her instinct then had been the right one?

'So you're planning on settling down in England?' she questioned, and then gave a nervous laugh. 'Though I guess you already are settled.'

There was brief pause as Tariq swirled a forkful of tagliatelli and coated it in sauce. But he didn't eat it. Instead, he lifted his eyes to hers, a sardonic smile curving his lips. It was always the same. Or rather women were. Didn't matter what you talked about, their careless chatter inevitably morphed into thinly veiled queries about his future. Because didn't they automatically daydream about *their* future and wonder if it could be a match with his? Weren't they programmed to do that, when they became the lover of a powerful alpha male?

'By "settling down", I suppose you mean getting married and having children?' he questioned.

Isobel nodded. 'I suppose so.'

Tariq's lips curved. She *supposed* so! 'The perfect nuclear family?'

'Well—'

'Which doesn't exist,' he interjected.

'That's a little harsh, Tariq.'

'Is it?' Black eyes iced into her. 'You experienced one yourself, did you?'

'Well, no. You know I didn't. I told you that I never knew my father.'

'And it left a gaping hole in your life?'

'I tried never to think of it that way,' she said defensively. 'Holes can always be filled by something else. It may not have been a "normal" family life, but it was a life.'

'Well, I never knew a "normal" childhood, either,' he said, more bitterly than he had intended.

'Can I…can I ask what happened?'

He stared at her, and she looked so damned sweet and soft that he found himself telling her. 'My mother almost died having me, and after I was born she was so ill that she needed round-the-clock care. Zahid was that bit older, and a calmer child than me, and it was decided that my needs were being neglected. So they sent me away to boarding school when I was seven. That's when I first came to England.'

Isobel frowned. She hadn't realised that he'd been so young. 'Wasn't there anywhere closer to home you could have gone?'

He shook his head. 'We have a completely different system of schooling in Khayarzah—it was decided that a western education would be beneficial all round.' He read the puzzlement in her tawny eyes. 'It meant that I would be able to speak and act like a westerner. More importantly, to think as a westerner thinks—which has proved invaluable in my subsequent business dealings. It's why the Al Hakam company has global domination,' he finished, with the flicker of a smile.

But, despite his proud smile, Isobel felt desperately

sad for him, even though she could see the logic behind
his parents' decision. She had been the daughter of a
school nurse and knew how illness could create chaos
in the most ordered of lives. Sending away a lively little
boy from his mother's sickbed must have seemed like a
sensible solution at the time.

Yet to move a child to live somewhere else—without any kind of family support nearby—and what did
that child become? A cuckoo in the nest in his adopted
country. And surely he must have felt like an outsider
whenever he returned to his homeland? Tariq had spoken the truth, she realised. He *didn't* have any place of
his own—not in any true sense of the word. Yes, there
were the apartments in London and New York, and the
luxury houses on Mustique and in the South of France—
but nowhere he could really call *home*. Not in his heart.

'So you don't ever want children of your own?' she
questioned boldly.

At this the shutters came down and his voice cooled.
'Not ever,' he affirmed, his gaze never leaving her
face—because she had to understand that he meant this.
'My brother has helpfully produced twin boys, and our
country now has the required heir and a spare. So my
assistance with dynasty-building is not required.'

A shiver ran down her spine as his unemotional words
registered. Was that what he thought fatherhood and
family life was all about...*dynasties?* Didn't he long
to hold his own little baby boy or girl in his arms? To
cradle them and to rock them? To see the past and the
future written in its tiny features?

She looked at his face in the candlelight. Such a
strong and indomitable face, she thought, with its high
slash of cheekbones, the hawk-like nose and wide, sen-

sual mouth. But behind the impressive physical package he presented she had discovered a reason for the unmistakable sense of *aloneness* which always seemed to surround him.

Yet this notoriously private man had actually confided in her. Surely that had to mean *something?* That he trusted her, yes—but was there anything more than that. And was it enough for her to face risking her heart?

She drifted her eyes over his hands—powerful and hair roughened. On the white silk cuffs of his shirt gleamed two heavy golden cufflinks. She could see that they were Khayarzah cufflinks, with the distinctive silhouette of a brooding falcon poised for flight. And somehow the bird of prey reminded her of him. Restless and seeking...above the world, but never really part of it.

Had he seen her looking at them? Was that why his hand suddenly reached out and caught hold of hers, capturing her wrist in his warm grasp and making it seem tiny and frail in comparison? His thumb brushed over the delicate skin at her wrist and he gave a brief smile as he felt the frantic skitter of her pulse.

'Stunned into uncharacteristic silence by my story, are you, Izzy?'

'It's some story,' she admitted quietly.

'Yes.' He looked down at her untouched plate. 'You're not eating.'

'Neither are you.'

'Delicious as it looks, I'm not feeling particularly hungry.'

'No.'

Across the candlelit table, their eyes met. 'Perhaps some fresh air might give us a little *appetite*.'

Isobel blinked at him in bewilderment. 'You want to go for a walk?'

His smile was wry. He'd forgotten that she had every right to be naïve, for she knew nothing of the games that lovers played... 'Only as far as the car. I thought we could go to my apartment. There's plenty of food there.'

Isobel's heart began to pound as his lazy suggestion shimmered into the space between them. She hadn't thought a lot beyond the meal itself. Somehow she had imagined that she might be going home alone to her little flat, as if the whole...*sex*...thing had been nothing but a distant dream. She'd told herself that would be the best for both of them, even if her commitment to the idea had been less than whole-hearted.

But then Tariq had opened up to her, taking her into his confidence. It had felt almost as intimate as when he'd been driving into her body. How could she possibly go home alone when she thought about the alternative he was offering her?

He was gesturing for the bill, seeming to take her silence for acquiescence, and the waiter was coming over to their table, his face creased in an anxious frown.

'You no like the food?' he questioned.

'The food is delicious,' Tariq replied, giving Isobel's hand a quick squeeze. 'I just find my partner's beauty rather distracting. So we'll just have the bill, please.'

Isobel saw the man-to-man look which passed between Tariq and the waiter, and for a moment she felt betrayed. Suddenly she had become someone else—not the woman who'd been frequenting this place for years, but someone dining with a man who was clearly way out of her league.

The waiter moved away, and Isobel tried to wriggle her fingers free. But Tariq wasn't having any of it.

'What's the matter, Izzy?'

'Just because you want to go to bed with me, it doesn't mean you have to tell lies!'

'Lies?' he questioned, perplexed.

'I am *not* beautiful,' she insisted.

'Oh, but you are,' he said unexpectedly, and then he did let go of her hand. Instead, he moved to cup her chin, running the tip of his thumb over it. 'Tonight you look very beautiful, sitting there, bathed in candlelight. I like your hair loose. I even like your eyes flashing with defiance. In fact, I can't quite remember ever seeing a woman look quite as desirable as you do right now, and it's making me ache for you. And you feel exactly the same, don't you?'

'Tariq!'

'Don't you?'

She met the mocking gleam in his ebony eyes. 'Yes,' she whispered.

'So pick up your handbag and let's get out of here— before I do something really crazy like hauling you to your feet and kissing you in front of the entire restaurant. Now, that really *would* provide fodder for the tabloids.'

She was trembling with anticipation as they went outside, where Tariq's chauffeur-driven car was sitting purring by the kerb. Climbing into its sumptuous interior, she waited for him to pull her into his arms. To kiss her as she so badly wanted to be kissed.

But he didn't. In fact he slid his body as far away from her as possible, and when he saw her turn her head he must have read the disappointed expression in her eyes because he shook his head.

'No, Izzy,' he said sternly. 'Not here and not now. I think we have demonstrated the wilder side of passion, and I think I've made it clear that once I start touching you all bets seem to be off. Tonight we will have the slow burn of anticipation and I will show you just how pleasurable *that* can be.'

Even when they reached his apartment he simply laced his fingers in hers and led her along the long corridor to his bedroom. Once there, with dexterous efficiency, he began to slide the clothes from her body. Only this time he hung her black silky dress over the back of a chair and did not tear off her panties.

When at last she was stripped bare, he peeled back the silken throw which covered his bed and laid her down on it.

'I want to see you naked,' he murmured appraisingly, as his gaze travelled slowly down the length of her body.

She watched as he undressed, the breath dying in her throat. His body was taut and magnificent—and he made no attempt to hide the heavy length of his arousal. But when at last he was completely naked, and maybe because he felt the trembling of her body, he frowned.

Smoothing back the cascade of Titian curls, he looked deep into her eyes. 'You are nervous?'

'A little.'

'But there is no reason to be, *habiba*.' He brushed his mouth over hers. 'For tonight there will be no pain—only endless pleasure.'

She gave herself up to his kiss at last, glad to lose herself in its seductive power. And grateful, too, for the clamour of her senses, which responded instantly to his expert touch and drove all nagging thoughts from her mind.

It was only afterwards that they came back to haunt her. When all passion was spent and they were lying there, Tariq's hand splayed possessively over the damp fuzz of curls at her thighs and her head slumped against his shoulder.

No pain, he had said—only pleasure.

But he had been talking about the physical pain of having surrendered her virginity to him. Not the infinitely more powerful pain she suspected might be about to be inflicted on her heart.

CHAPTER EIGHT

The office door clicked quietly shut, and Tariq's distinctively soft voice whispered over Isobel's senses.

'So what has it been like without me, *kalila?* Did the office grind to a halt without me? More importantly... did you miss your Sheikh while he was away?'

Isobel looked up from her work, trying to steel herself against the impact of seeing Tariq for the first time in almost a week. Having to fight back the urge to do something stupid—like leaping up and throwing herself into his arms.

He'd been to New York on business, and along the way had taken delivery of a new transatlantic jet. He'd also announced the expansion of the Al Hakam Bank in Singapore, but was still refusing to confirm reports that he was in the process of buying the famous 'Blues' football team. Consequently, his face had been pictured on the front pages of the financial press—and Isobel had secretly pored over them whenever she had a spare moment. It had felt slightly peculiar to look at the hard and handsome face which stared back at her amid the newsprint. And to realise that the man with the hawk-like features and noble lineage was actually her lover.

Now he leaned over her desk, a vision of alpha-sexiness in a dark grey suit and pristine white shirt. His olive skin made him look as if he had been cast in gold, and his black eyes gleamed as they surveyed her questioningly.

'Tariq,' she said slowly, laying down her pen and putting the churned up feeling in her stomach down to his tantalising proximity. 'You know perfectly well that the office always runs smoothly in your absence. In fact, there's a quiet air of calm around the place. People are that bit more relaxed when the big boss isn't around.'

He gave a slow smile as he loosened his tie and dropped it in front of her like a calling card. She sounded as unruffled as she always did when she spoke to him in the office—her cool air of composure barely slipping. Why, nobody would guess that the last time they'd seen each other she had been giving him oral sex in the back of his darkened limousine. Demonstrating yet another new-found sexual skill which she seemed to have adopted with her usual dexterity.

And he had reciprocated by sliding his fingers beneath her skirt and bringing her to a shuddering orgasm just moments before he'd left the car to catch his flight to JFK.

Yet to look at her now she seemed light-years away from his fevered and erotic memory of her. She looked restrained and efficient—almost *prim.*

To Tariq's surprise, any fears he'd had that she would become cloying or demanding had not been realised. Despite being such a sexual novice, Izzy seemed to have no problems juggling her dual roles as his lover and PA, and was as discreet as anyone in his position could have wished for.

He frowned. The only downside was that she seemed

to be getting underneath his skin in a way he hadn't anticipated. By now he should have been growing a little bored with her—because that was his pattern. Once the gloss of new sex had worn off, predictability tended to set in—and three weeks was usually long enough for him to begin to find out things about a woman which irritated him.

But Izzy was different, and he wasn't quite sure why. Might it be because she knew him better than almost anyone? Working so closely with him over the years had given her glimpses of the private person that he would never have allowed another to see. Sometimes it felt as though she had already stripped away several layers to see the man who lay beneath. Was that what gave sex with her its extra dimension of closeness? Or was it just the fearless way she responded to him? The way she looked straight into his eyes while he was deep inside her? As if she wanted to see into his soul with those big tawny eyes of hers. Sometimes it unsettled him and sometimes it did not—but it always excited him.

He watched as she picked up his discarded tie and began to roll it into a neat silken coil. 'So, did you miss me?' he repeated.

Isobel put the tie down and looked at him. What would he do if she told him that she *always* missed him? That she wished she could suddenly become one of his ties, so that she could wrap herself round his neck all day and stay there? He would run a million miles away—that was what he would do. Declarations of adoration were not what Tariq wanted, but she could see perfectly well from his darkening eyes just what he *did* want.

She rose from her desk and walked towards him,

aware of his gaze on her and conscious of the fact that her thighs were bare above her stocking tops. She'd dressed with deliberate daring for the office this morning, knowing that he was bound to want her as soon as he arrived—and determined to feed into the fantasies he had assured her on the phone last night had been building all week.

She might be new to all this, but some survival instinct had made her turn herself into the best lover she could possibly be. Because wasn't that her default method? To do something to the best of her ability? Didn't that usually mean security? If you became so good at something then you wouldn't be replaced.

Only this wasn't a new job, or a new project which was going to enhance her life. This was all about a relationship—it was strange new territory. Her mother's often repeated warnings still came to her from time to time, but how could she take them seriously when she was looking into the glittering hunger of Tariq's black eyes and feeling the lurch of her heart in response?

'Of course I've missed you,' she said softly.

'How much, on a scale of one to ten?'

'Well...' She pretended to think about it. 'How about seven?'

'Seven?'

'Eight, then. Nine! *Tariq!* Okay—ten!'

'You're wearing *stockings,*' he breathed in disbelief.

'Well, you've nagged me often enough about my tights.'

'With good reason. Let me see.' He lifted up her skirt and expelled a small appraising sigh. The tops of the dark silk stockings had been embroidered with deep turquoise and green, so that it looked as if some peacock had wrapped its feathers enticingly around her thighs and left them there. 'You know that there are consequences to dressing like that?' he questioned unsteadily.

'What kind of consequences might they be?'

'Can't you guess?' he breathed, as he placed her hand on the fly of his trousers.

'T-Tariq.'

'I want you, Izzy.'

'You always want me,' she whispered back, her fingertips caressing the thick, hard shaft.

He swallowed. 'And is it mutual?'

'You know it is.'

He caught her by the shoulders and looked down into her widened tawny eyes. 'Then why don't you show me how much you've missed me?' he questioned unsteadily. 'Because I have missed you too, *kalila*.'

She savoured his unsteady words as she rose up on tiptoe to kiss him, revelling in the sheer pleasure of being in his arms again. She closed her eyes as his practised fingers began to reacquaint themselves with her body. At times like this, when he could reduce her to boneless longing within seconds, it was easy to imagine that a unique bond existed between them. Was that because they seemed to have the ability to anticipate each other's needs—despite the disparity of their experience—or was it because they simply knew each other so well?

Or was it something far more commonplace? He'd told her candidly that making love without having to wear a condom was the biggest turn-on he'd ever known. For him, that was a brand-new experience, and that was rare enough to excite a man who'd been having sex since he was a teenager. She'd tried telling herself that

Tariq's reaction to her was purely physical. Because if she looked the truth straight in the face then surely there was less likelihood of her getting hurt?

If only her own feelings were as straightforward. If only she hadn't started to care. Really care. She wondered if it was normal for a woman to become a little more emotionally vulnerable every time her man made love to her. For her to start wanting things she knew she wasn't supposed to want—things he'd specifically warned her against? Things that Tariq was renowned for never delivering—and especially to a woman like her. Stuff like commitment and happy-ever-after.

'Izzy?'

She closed her eyes, letting go of the last of her troubled thoughts, allowing pure and delicious sensation to take over instead. 'Yes,' she whispered, as he pushed her down onto the floor and sank down beside her. 'Oh, yes.'

His fingers were on her flesh now, stroking open the moist and heated flesh at the very core of her, and he was saying, *Luloah...* softly and fervently beneath his breath, something which Isobel had learnt meant 'pearl' in his native tongue.

'You taste of honey,' he said on a shuddered breath, his mouth high on her thigh.

'Tariq—' His tongue had reached the most sensitive part of her anatomy, and Isobel gave a little gasp of pleasure as she felt its delicate flick. Glancing down, she could see the erotic image of her boss's black head between her legs, and the sheer intimacy of it only increased the sensations which were beginning to ripple through her.

Her head fell back as an unstoppable heat began to

build, and she trembled on the brink as he teased her with his tongue.

'Tariq,' she gasped again, clutching at his shoulders, her fingers biting into him.

'What?' he drawled against her heated flesh.

Tariq, I think I'm falling in love with you!

But her passionate thoughts dissolved as a feeling of intense pleasure washed over her—strong enough to sweep away everything else in its wake. Wave after wave of it racked her trembling body—and just when she thought it couldn't get any better he thrust deep inside her.

'You feel so *good,*' he said unsteadily.

'So...do you.'

He thrust even deeper, his breaths becoming long and shuddering. 'And I've been wanting to do this to you *all week.*'

She heard his voice change and felt his body tense, watched him splinter with his own pleasure. She loved the helplessness of his orgasm, feeling in those few heightened moments of sensation that he was really hers.

Afterwards, they lay wrapped tightly in each other's arms, until Isobel lifted her head to free some of the hair which was trapped beneath his elbow.

'You know, we're going to have to stop meeting like this,' she murmured.

Tariq laughed , drawing his fingers through the spill of her curls and marvelling at how *uncomplicated* all this seemed. His mouth settled into a curve of satisfaction. He could walk in from a trip and within minutes have her writhing and compliant in his arms. There were no demands made, nor questions asked. What could be better than that?

'I think this is a very good place to meet.' He yawned. 'You've brought a whole new meaning to the expression "job satisfaction".'

But Isobel wasn't really listening. Now that her euphoric state had begun to evaporate she was remembering what she'd been thinking at the height of their lovemaking. About loving him.

She stared at the ceiling, her heart beginning to pound with fear. *Love?* Surely she wasn't crazy enough to waste an emotion like that on a man who very definitely didn't want it? Who had explicitly warned her against it? And hadn't her mother done the very same? She'd managed to convince her daughter that love was rare—and Isobel knew it was an impossibility to expect it from a seasoned playboy who shied away from commitment.

Uncomfortably, she wriggled, wanting to get away, to try and soothe her confused thoughts into some kind of order. 'Tariq, we can't lie here all day.'

'Why not? We can do anything we like.' He touched his lips to hers. 'I *am* the boss.'

She pulled away from him—but not before he had caught hold of her, his eyes narrowed. 'Something is wrong, *kalila?*' he queried softly. 'You are angry with me because we have had yet another *fumble* on the floor of the office?'

Isobel smiled. 'I can hardly blame you for wanting instant sex when I was a willing participant. I just happen to know that there's a whole pile of things which need your attention. And we *are* supposed to be working.'

Yawning, he rose to his feet and held out a hand. 'By

the way—I've brought you a present from New York,'
he said as he pulled to her feet.

'Oh?' She felt her heart skip a beat. 'It's not my birth-
day.'

"That's a little disingenuous of you, Izzy.' Walking
over to his briefcase, he slanted her a lazy smile as he
withdrew a slim leather case. 'Don't you like presents?'

She wasn't sure—her feelings were pretty mixed
when it came to presents from Tariq. She wanted to be
the first and only woman he'd ever bought a gift for. Not
to feel as if she was just one in a long line of women who
smiled their acceptance of whatever glittering trinket he
had bought them. *But she was. That was exactly what
she was.*

She wanted to tell him that she didn't need presents.
Because she knew him too well and she knew how he
operated. Her counterpart in New York had probably
been dispatched to choose something for her—just as
she had chosen such gifts for his lovers many times before. She had probably even consulted him to find out
what the budget for such a gift should be.

But she kept silent. She was curious and scared,
knowing that she was in no position to make highly
charged pronouncements because of what the outcome
might be. Because mightn't he just shrug his shoulders
and walk away?

So she took the box he handed her and flipped open
the clasp with fingers which were miraculously steady.
The first irreverent thought which crossed her mind
was that she was pretty low down on the price scale.
After five years of choosing various sparklers for Tariq's
women, she could see instantly that her own offering

would not have caused a stratospheric hole in his wallet. No diamonds or emeralds for *her.*

But in a stupid way she was glad. Precious jewels would have been all wrong on someone like her: they would have felt like some sort of *payment* and they wouldn't have suited her. Instead Tariq had bought her something she might actually have saved up for and bought for herself.

Lying on bed of blue-black velvet lay a shoal of opals, fashioned into in a dramatic waterfall of a necklace. Isobel drew it out of the box. The stones were dark grey—almost black—but as the necklace shimmered over her fingers she could see the transformation of each gem into a vivid rainbow.

'Do you like it?' questioned Tariq.

Isobel blinked. 'It's the most beautiful thing I've ever seen,' she whispered.

'I chose it myself,' he said unexpectedly. 'I liked the element of surprise. In some lights it looks quite subdued—while in other aspects it's amazingly vibrant.' His eyes narrowed and his tone was dry. 'A little like you, in fact, Izzy.'

Isobel suddenly became extremely preoccupied with the jewellery, swallowing down the glimmer of tears which were hovering at the back of her eyes. He'd chosen it himself. To her certain knowledge he'd never done that before—not in all the time she'd worked for him. So did that *mean* anything? She couldn't help the wild leap of her heart. Did such an unexpected gesture mean that his feelings for her might be growing and changing? Dared she...dared she *hope* for such a thing?

'You do like it, Izzy?'

His question broke into her thoughts and she lifted her head. 'I do like it. In fact, I *love* it.'

'Good.' There was a pause. 'I thought you might want to wear it tomorrow night.'

She heard the studied casualness in his voice. 'Why? What's happening tomorrow night?'

'My brother is in town.'

She blinked. 'You mean your brother, the *King?*'

'I only have one brother,' he answered drily. 'He flew my sister-in-law to Paris for their wedding anniversary. Francesca hasn't been back in England in nearly a year, so they've decided to come on to London. Our embassy is throwing a formal dinner for them tonight—which I shall have to attend. But tomorrow they want to meet up privately. You've spoken to Zahid on the phone so many times that I thought you might like this opportunity to meet him.'

Carefully, she put the necklace back in its case and smiled. 'I'd love to meet your brother,' she said.

'Good.' Tariq walked through to his private office, calling out over his shoulder, 'I'll let you have the details later.'

Isobel waited until the door had closed behind him, then stared at the jewellery case in her handbag, a strange cocktail of emotions forming a tight knot at the pit of her stomach. She might be going out of her mind, but try as she might she couldn't quite subdue the sudden flare of happiness which rose within her. Hand-picked jewels and meeting his brother were surely remarkable enough to merit a little analysis. Was it possible that, deep down, Tariq was willing to move this relationship on to something a little more tangible?

Cold reason tried to swamp her as she remembered

the emphatic way he'd told her that he didn't ever want commitment, or a family of his own. But measured against that was the terrible loneliness he'd experienced as a child. Maybe now he was coming to realise that people could change—and so could circumstances. That what they had was good. That it didn't have to peter out after a few weeks—that maybe it could endure and grow. Was that too much to hope for?

But she felt as if she was on shifting sands—her hopes quickly replaced by a strange feeling of foreboding as she remembered something she'd read somewhere.

She clicked open the box to stare at the multi-hued fire of her brand-new necklace, and frowned. Because weren't opals supposed to be awfully *unlucky?*

CHAPTER NINE

'You look *fine,* Izzy. Really.'

For the umpteenth time Isobel smoothed damp palms down over her thick mass of curls, aware that she was probably mussing her hair up instead of flattening it. She frowned at Tariq. What kind of a recommendation was that? 'Fine' wasn't the kind of description she wanted when she was about to meet the King of Khayarzah and his English bride Queen Francesca. Not when she felt so nervous that her knees were actually shaking.

'That's a pretty lukewarm endorsement,' she said.

His black eyes gleamed as he captured one of her fluttering hands and directed it towards his mouth. 'I thought honesty was our mantra?'

'Maybe it is, but sometimes a woman needs a little fabrication.'

'No need for fabrication, *kalila,*' he said. He brushed her a brief kiss as their car drew to a halt outside the glittering frontage of the Granchester Hotel, but if the truth were known he was finding this very feminine need for reassurance a touch too *domestic* for his taste. Had it been wise to extend this invitation? he wondered. Or was Izzy now reading far more into it than he'd intended her to read? Maybe he should have made it clearer that there was no real significance behind the meeting with his brother. 'You look absolutely stunning,' he drawled. 'Didn't I tell you exactly that just an hour ago?'

Yes, he had, Isobel conceded. But a man said all kinds of things to a woman when he had just finished ravishing her in the middle of his big bed...

Their spontaneous lovemaking had left her running late—but maybe it was better not to have had time to fret about her appearance when she'd been nervous enough already. She was wearing a new dress in grey silk jersey, and its careful draping did amazing things for her figure. She'd teamed the dress with high-heeled black suede shoes, and on Tariq's instructions had left her hair hanging loose. She'd wondered aloud if the wild cloud of Titian curls was not a little too much, but he had wound his fingers through its corkscrew strands and told her that it was a crime to hide it away.

Her only adornment was the opals he had brought her back from America, and they sparkled rainbow light at her throat and dominated the subdued palette of her outfit. *The gems he'd chosen for her himself...* How could such beautiful gems possibly be unlucky? she asked herself, her fingertips reaching up to touch the cool stones as a doorman sprang to open the car door.

The private elevator zoomed them up to the penthouse suite, and when the door was opened by a man who was unmistakably Tariq's brother all Isobel's expectations were confounded.

He had the same hawk-like features as Tariq—and the same knockout combination of ebony hair and glowing olive skin. But he was casually dressed in dark trousers, and although he was wearing a silk shirt he was tieless. Isobel had been expecting to be greeted by a servant, so her curtsey was hastily scrambled together and ill-prepared. But King Zahid smiled at her as he indicated that she should rise.

'No formality,' he warned. 'That is my wife's instruction, and I dare not disobey!'

'Why, Zahid—you sound as if you are almost under the thumb,' mocked Tariq softly.

'Perhaps I am. And a very beautiful thumb it happens to be,' murmured Zahid.

'You've changed,' observed Tariq, creasing his brow in a frown. 'You'd never have admitted to something like that in the past.'

'Ah, but everything changes, Tariq,' said Zahid. 'That is one of life's great certainties.'

For a moment the light of challenge sparked between the eyes of the brothers, and for a moment Isobel caught a glimpse of what the two men must have been like as children.

'Come this way,' continued Zahid, leading them into an enormous sitting room whose floor-to-ceiling windows overlooked the park.

And there, with a baby on her knee and another crawling close by on the floor, was the English Queen Francesca, her dark hair tied back in a ponytail and a slightly harassed smile on her face. She had a snowy blanket hanging over one shoulder, and was holding a grubby white toy polar bear, at which the sturdy baby on her lap kept lunging.

Isobel blinked. The last thing she'd expected was to see a queen in blue jeans, playing nursemaid!

'No, please don't curtsey, Izzy—we're very relaxed here,' said Francesca with a wide smile. 'But if you want to be really helpful you could pick up Omar before he tries to eat Zahid's shoe! Azzam has already tried! Darling, I do wish you'd keep them out of reach.'

Rather nervously, Isobel bent to scoop up the black-haired baby, aware that one of these precious boy twins was the heir to the Khayarzah throne. A robust little creature, Omar was wearing an exquisite yellow romper suit which contrasted with his ebony curls. He took one long and suspicious look at the woman now holding him, then gave a shout as he began to tug at her hair.

Isobel giggled as she extricated his tiny chubby fingers, all the nerves she'd been feeling suddenly evaporating. You couldn't possibly feel uptight when you were holding a cuddly bundle like this. He was so *sweet!* She risked a glance at Tariq, but met no answering smile on his face. In fact his expression suddenly looked so *glacial* that she felt momentarily flummoxed. But at least he was now directing the chilly stare at his brother instead of her.

'Don't you have any nannies with you?' Tariq asked Zahid coolly.

'Not one,' answered Zahid, giving his wife a long and indulgent look. 'Francesca decided that she wanted us to have a "normal" family holiday—just like other people.'

'And you agreed?' questioned Tariq incredulously.

'Actually, I find that I'm enjoying the experience,' said Zahid. 'It's useful to be "hands-on".'

'I want our children to know their parents,' said Francesca firmly. 'Not to be brought out like ornaments, for best. Zahid, aren't you going to offer our guests a drink?'

Isobel saw Tariq's face darken. Clearly he did *not* approve of the babies being present, and she noticed that he kept as far away from his nephews as possible. She wondered how he could possibly ignore such cute little black-haired dumplings, before deciding that it was *his* problem and that she was just going to relax and enjoy herself.

In fact the evening went much better than she could have hoped. She took turns cuddling both Omar and Azzam, and ended up kicking off her high-heeled shoes and helping Francesca bath the twins in one of the fancy *en-suite* bathrooms. Her dove-grey dress was soon splattered with drops of water, but she didn't care.

They grappled to dress the wriggling boys in animal-dotted sleepsuits, and then brought them in to the men to say goodnight, all warm and rosy and smelling delicious. But she noticed that Tariq's embrace was strictly perfunctory as each baby was offered up to him for a kiss.

She tried not to be unsettled by his rather forbidding body language as she and Francesca carried the babies through to the bedroom and laid them down in their two little cots. For a while they stood watching as two sets of heavily hooded eyes drooped down into exhausted sleep, and then—as if colluding in some wonderful secret—both women smiled at each other.

Francesca bent to tuck the polar bear next to Azzam, then straightened up. 'You know, we've never met any of Tariq's girlfriends before,' she said.

Isobel wasn't quite sure how to respond. She didn't really *feel* like his girlfriend—more like an employee, with benefits. But she could hardly confess that to the Sheikh's sister-in-law, could she? Or start explaining the exact nature of those 'benefits'? Instead, she smiled.

'I'm very honoured to be here,' she answered quietly.

Francesca hesitated. 'Sometimes Zahid worries about Tariq. He thinks that surely there's only so much living in the fast lane one person can do. It would be nice to see him settle down at last.'

Now Isobel felt a complete fraud, because she knew very well that Tariq had no intention of settling down. Not with her—and not with anyone. He'd made that more than clear. Because when a man told you unequivocally that he never wanted children he was telling you something big, wasn't he? Something you couldn't really ignore. And if she'd been labouring under any illusion that he hadn't meant it—well, she'd discovered tonight that he had. With his stony countenance and disapproving air, he'd made it pretty clear that children didn't do it for him.

And if Zahid and Francesca thought that her appearance here was anything more than expedient—that she and Tariq were about to start playing happy-ever-after—well, they were in for a big disappointment.

'I don't know whether some men are ever quite ready to settle down,' she told the Queen diplomatically. 'He isn't known as the Playboy Prince for nothing!'

Francesca opened her mouth as if she wanted to say something else, but clearly thought better of it because she shut it again. 'Come on,' she said. 'Let's go and eat dinner. I want to hear all about life in England—the fashion, the films. Who's dating who. What's big on TV. I get a whole load of stuff off the internet, of course, but it's never quite the same.'

And Isobel nodded and smiled, feeling an immense sense of relief that the subject of Tariq's inability to commit had been terminated.

Dinner was served in the lavish dining room which

led off the main room, its table covered in snowy linen and decorated with white fragrant flowers. Heavy silver cutlery reflected the light which guttered from tall, creamy candles, and the overall effect was one of restrained luxury and taste.

'This looks wonderful,' said Isobel shyly, realising that this was the first time she'd been given an insider's experience of Tariq's royal life.

'A dinner fit for a king!' said Francesca, and they all laughed as they took their places around the table.

The evening passed in a bit of a blur. Isobel was aware of being served the most amazing food, but it was mostly wasted on her. She might as well have been eating bread and butter for all the notice she took of the exquisite fare. She could hardly believe she was here with Tariq—meeting his family like this. It had the heady but disconcerting effect of almost *normalising* their relationship—and she knew that was a dangerous way to start thinking. Just because you really wanted something, it didn't necessarily mean it was going to happen.

So she joined in as much as she could, though she felt completely lost when the two brothers began speaking in their own language.

'They're discussing the new trade deal with Maraban,' confided Francesca.

Isobel put her knife and fork down. 'Do you speak any Khayarzahian?' she questioned.

'Only a little. I'm learning all the time—though it's not the easiest language in the world. But I'm determined to be fluent one day—just as my sons will be.'

'They're such beautiful babies,' said Isobel, a sudden note of wistfulness entering her voice almost before she'd realised.

'Not getting broody, are you?' Francesca laughed.

It was perhaps unfortunate that the brothers' conversation chose that precise moment to end and Tariq glanced up. He must have heard what they'd been saying, Isobel thought, her skin suddenly growing cold with fear. He *must* have done. Why else did he fix her with an expression she'd never seen before? A calculating look iced the ebony depths of his eyes which made her feel like some sort of gatecrasher.

'Of course I'm not!' she denied quickly, reaching for a glass of water and horribly aware of the sudden flush of colour to her cheeks. Why was he looking at her like that—with his eyes full of suspicion? Did he think she was trying to ingratiate herself with the monarch and his wife? Or did he think she really *was* getting broody?

One moment she had been part of their charmed inner circle—warmed by its privileged light—and now in an instant it felt as if she had been kicked out and left to shiver on the darkened sidelines.

By the time the evening ended her feeling of despondency had grown—though she managed to maintain her bright air of enjoyment until the car door had closed on them and they were once more locked within its private space.

She settled back in the seat, unable to shake off the feeling of having been judged and found wanting, aware that Tariq did not slide his arm around her shoulder and draw her closer to him. And suddenly she was reminded of that very first time she'd had sex with him. When she'd been driven home—knickerless and confused— after first dropping him off at the Maraban Embassy.

Back then she had been painfully aware of him keeping her at a distance, and he was doing it again now.

Even though in the intervening weeks they had been lovers it was almost like being transported back in time. Because nothing had really changed, had it? Not for Tariq. She might be guilty of concocting fast-growing fantasies about how hand-chosen pieces of jewellery meant that he was starting to care for her—but that was just wishful thinking. Like some young girl who read her horoscope and then prayed it would come true.

'You seemed to be getting on very well with Francesca,' he observed, his voice breaking into her thoughts.

'I hope I did all right?' she questioned, telling herself that any woman in her position would have asked the same question.

'I thought you carried it off superbly.'

'Thanks,' she said uncertainly.

But Tariq leaned back in his seat, unable to dispel the growing sense of unease inside him. The whole evening had unsettled him, and it wasn't difficult to work out why. Zahid in jeans—with no help for the children—and in a hotel suite which looked as if it had just been burgled.

He shook his head in faint disbelief. It was scarcely credible to him that his once so formal and slightly stuffy older brother was now like putty in the hands of his wife.

But it hadn't just been the sense of chaos which had unsettled him. Something about their close family unit had opened up the dark space which was buried deep in Tariq's heart. Watching his brother playing with his children had reinforced his sense of feeling like an outsider. Always the outsider.

He shot Isobel a glance, remembering the way their

gazes had met over the dark curly head of his nephew. Had that been wistfulness he'd read in her eyes as she'd held the baby in her arms? Was she doing that clucky thing which seemed to happen to all women, no matter how much they tried to deny it? Especially if they knew that a man was watching them...

But why *shouldn't* she long for babies of her own? That was what women were conditioned to do. The most unforgivable thing would be for a man who didn't want children to waste the time of a woman who *did*.

He saw that her eyes were now closed. Her cheeks looked as smooth as marble. Her grey dress and the new opals were muted in the subdued light of the car. Only her magnificent mane of hair provided glowing life and colour. And suddenly, in this quiet place, all the things he usually blotted out came crowding into his mind.

He hadn't given any thought to the future. He hadn't planned this affair with Izzy—it had just sprung up, out of the blue, and been surprisingly good. But sooner or later something had to give. It wasn't for ever. His relationships never were. And the longer it went on, then surely the more it would fill her with false hope. She might start seeing a happy-ever-after for them both— which was never going to happen. Wasn't it better and more honest to end it now, before he really hurt her—a woman he liked and respected far too much to ever want to hurt?

He realised that she had fallen asleep, and although a part of him wanted to lean over and wake her with a kiss he reminded himself that this wasn't a fairytale.

He was not that prince.

Gently, he shook her shoulder, and her big, tawny eyes snapped open.

'Wake up, Izzy,' he said softly.

'What's the matter?' Groggily, she sat up and looked around. 'Are we nearly home?'

It was her choice of word which helped make his mind up. Because for them there was no 'home' and there never would be. She had her place and he had his—and maybe it was time to start drawing a clear line between the two.

'I'm going to get the car to drop me off,' he said softly. 'And then the driver will take you on to your apartment.'

Isobel snuggled up to him. 'Don't be silly,' she murmured. 'I'll come home with you.'

There it was again—that seemingly innocuous word which now seemed weighted down with all kinds of heavy meaning.

'Not tonight, Izzy. I have to take a conference call very early tomorrow, and it's pointless the two of us being woken up.' Lightly he brushed his lips over hers before drawing away—before the sweet taste of her could tempt him into changing his mind—glad that the limousine was now drawing up outside his apartment. 'And, thanks to you, I got very little sleep last night.'

Feeling stupidly rejected, Isobel nodded. In a way, his explanation made things worse. It made her feel as if she was *wanting* something from him and he was withholding it.

Or was she simply tired and imagining things? Maybe it would be better all round if she *did* go home alone. She could have an undisturbed night's sleep, and tomorrow morning she would wake up bright and cheerful.

And everything would be the same as it had been before.

'Yes, we could probably *both* do with a good night's

sleep,' she said, keeping her voice resolutely cheerful. 'I'll see you in the morning.'

But as Tariq got out of the car she saw the sudden shuttering of his face, and she couldn't shift the sinking certainty that something between them had changed.

And changed for the worst.

CHAPTER TEN

So it was true.

Horribly, horribly true.

Isobel's fears that Tariq was *cooling* towards her were not some warped figment of her imagination, after all. She was getting the cool treatment. Definitely. She recognised it much too well to be mistaken.

She hadn't spent a night with him in almost a week even though he'd been in the same country—the same city, even. Every night there was another reason why he couldn't see her. He was eating out with a group of American bankers. Or meeting up with a friend who'd just flown in from Khayarzah. And even though his reasons sounded perfectly legitimate, Isobel couldn't shift the certainty that he was avoiding her.

These days, even when he came into the office, he seemed distracted. There was barely a good morning kiss. No smouldering look to send her pulse rate soaring and have her anticipating what might happen later. It was as if the Isobel she had been—the woman he desired and lusted after—was disappearing. She felt as if the old, invisible Isobel had returned to take her place. As if a switch had been flicked in Tariq's mind and it would never be the same again.

She tried telling herself it was because he was busy—but deep down she suspected a different reason for his distance. After all, she'd seen it happen countless times before, with other women. One minute they were flavour of the month, and the next they were like unwanted leftovers, lying congealed on the side of the plate.

The question was, what was she going to do about it? Was she going to sit back and let him push her away—gradually chipping at her already precarious self-esteem—until she was left with nothing? Or was she going to be proactive enough to reach out and take control of her life? Should she just face up to him and ask whether they were to consign their affair to memory?

Until she realised that Tariq's apparent lack of interest was the least of her worries. And that there were some things which were of far more pressing concern...

She told herself that the nausea she was experiencing was a residual from the brief burst of sickness she'd had, caused by some rogue fish she'd eaten. That the slight aching in her breasts was due to her hormones, nothing else. She was on the pill, wasn't she? And the pill was blissfully safe. Everyone knew that.

But the feeling of nausea began to worsen, and so did the aching in her breasts. And then Tariq said something which made her think that perhaps she *wasn't* imagining it...

It happened that weekend, when she was staying over at his apartment. It seemed ages since they'd spent two whole days together, and she loved being there when they didn't have work the next day. It was the closest she ever felt to him—as if she was a real girlfriend, rather than a secretary who had just got lucky.

It was early on the Sunday morning that he made his

observation. Half-asleep, he had begun to kiss her, his hands to caress her breasts, and she had given a little sigh and nestled back against the soft bank of pillows.

'Izzy?' he murmured. 'Have you put on a little weight, do you think?'

She stiffened beneath the practised caress of his fingers. 'Why?' she blurted out. 'Do you think I'm getting fat?'

'There's no need to be so defensive.' He blew softly onto the hollow of her breastbone. 'You're slender enough to carry a few extra pounds. Men like curves—I've told you that before.'

But his words only increased her sense of anxiety, and she was almost relieved when the phone in his study began ringing and he swore a little before going off to answer it. It was the one phone he never ignored—the private line between him and his brother's palace in Khayarzah.

Isobel could hear him speaking in a lowered voice, so she took the opportunity to head for the bathroom down the corridor—the one he never used. Her heart was racing as she closed the door, and the terrible taste of fear was in her mouth. And she knew that she could no longer put off the moment of truth.

She flinched as she saw the image which was reflected back at her in the full-length mirror. Her face was paper-pale and her eyes looked huge and haunted, but it was her body which disturbed her. Like most women, she was not usually given to staring at her naked self, but even she could see that her breasts looked swollen and the nipples were much darker than usual.

Was she pregnant? *Was* she?

For a moment she lowered her head, to gaze at the

pristine white surface of the washbasin. She remembered how unequivocal Tariq had been about not wanting children—and clearly it hadn't been an idle declaration. Hadn't she witnessed for herself how cold he could be when he was around them? Why, he'd barely touched Omar or Azzam the other day—he'd seemed completely unmoved by their presence when everyone else had been cooing around them.

She wanted to sink to her knees and pray for some kind of miracle. But she couldn't afford to have hysterics or to act rashly. She needed time to think, and she needed to stay calm.

Quickly, she showered and put on jeans and a shirt, feeling the slight tug as she fastened the buttons across her chest.

The silence in the apartment told her that Tariq had finished his conversation, and in bare feet she padded along the corridor to find him standing in his study. He was staring out of the window, his powerful body silhouetted against the dramatic view.

When he turned round, he didn't comment on the fact that she had showered and dressed. A couple of weeks ago he would have growled his displeasure and started removing her clothes immediately, but not now—and a wave of regret washed over her for something between them which seemed to be lost.

'Is anything wrong?' she questioned.

He stared at her, his eyes focussing on her pale skin and anxious eyes, and a heavy sense of sadness enveloped him. What had happened to his smart and wise-cracking Izzy? He felt the heavy beat of guilt, aware of the enormity of what he had done. In typical Tariq fashion he had seen and he had conquered. Selfishly, he had listened to the voracious demands of his body and taken her as his lover, refusing to acknowledge the thoughtlessness of such an action.

She had been too inexperienced to resist the powerful lure of lust when it had swept over them so unexpectedly. *He* should have known better and *he* should have resisted. But he had not. He had done what he always did—he had taken and taken, knowing that he had nothing to give back.

And now he was left with the growing suspicion that he was going to lose the best assistant he'd ever had. For how could they carry on like this, when much of her natural spontaneity seemed to have been eroded by the affair?

He could tell that something had changed. It was as if she was walking on eggshells. He noticed that she kept biting back her words—which usually meant that a woman was falling in love with him, that she was weighing up everything she said for fear of how he would interpret it. And all these negative feelings would snowball—he knew that, too. How could he possibly face her in the office if her reproachful looks were to continue and the gap between them widened daily?

'Tariq?'

Her soft voice broke into his troubled thoughts. 'What?'

'I wondered if anything was wrong.'

'Wrong?'

She looked at him questioningly, telling herself that it was her business to know what was going on his life. But deep down she wanted to clear that scary look of distraction from his face. To have him *talk* to her. Properly.

'The phone call you've just had from Khayarzah?'

she elaborated. 'I hope everything's okay with your brother?'

With an effort, he focussed on the conversation he'd just finished. 'Zahid wants my help with a relative of ours.'

'Oh?'

'A distant cousin of mine, from my mother's side,' he explained. 'Her name is Leila, and she's in trouble.'

Isobel's face blanched as she wondered if the gods were taunting her. Because hadn't that expression always been a euphemism for a particular *kind* of predicament in which a woman sometimes found herself? Was it possible that a cruel fate was about to inflict not one but *two* unplanned pregnancies on the al Hakam family?

'Trouble?' she questioned hoarsely. 'What kind of trouble?'

'It seems she's decided she wants to junk university and go off to America to be a model. Can you imagine?' He gave a grim smile. 'Zahid thinks that she needs to be shown the error of her ways, and he thinks that I may just be able to sort things out.'

'I see.' Isobel nodded. Was she imagining the relief on his face—as if he was anticipating an adventure which would fully occupy him for the foreseeable future? As if he was pleased to have a *bone fide* reason to unexpectedly leave the country? 'Why does he think that?'

'He says that my uniquely western perspective might help persuade her. That I've seen enough of that kind of world to convince her that it's all starvation and cigarettes and people who will try to exploit her.' He shrugged. 'Nothing that need concern you—but I'm going to fly out later tonight, if you could make sure the new jet is ready for me?'

Two things occurred to her at the same time. The first was that he still came and went exactly as he pleased—becoming her lover had not curtailed his freedom in any way at all. And the second was that she knew there was no way she could announce her momentous news. Not when he was about to go on some mission of mercy for his brother. Not when she hadn't even had it confirmed. And until she did then surely there was always the chance that it was nothing but a false alarm?

But her decision didn't give her any peace of mind. She was still left with nagging doubts. Tariq was leaving to go back to his homeland, and suddenly she didn't know where her place in his life should be. She struggled to a find common ground.

'Did…did your brother and his wife enjoy themselves in London last week?' she asked.

'I assume so.'

'They didn't mention it?'

He raised dark brows. 'Should they have done?'

'Just…well, I thought it was quite a fun evening, that's all.'

'Indeed it was.' He gave a brief smile, preoccupied with his forthcoming trip and pleased to have something to take his mind of the damned tension between them. 'But they have a hectic life, you know, Izzy. Pretty much wall-to-wall socialising wherever they are.'

It was the hint of aloofness in his tone which made Isobel stiffen. That and the patronising sense that she had stepped over some invisible line of propriety. As if she had *dared* to look on the King and his wife as some sort of equals, instead of people she'd been lucky enough to meet only on a whim of Tariq's.

'Silly of me,' she said lightly.

There was a pause as she forced herself to acknowledge the tension which had sprung up between them and which now seemed there all the time. She didn't know when exactly it had happened, but it wouldn't seem to go away. Like a pebble dropped into a pond, the ripples carried on for ages after the stone had plopped out of sight.

She knew what was going on because she'd witnessed it countless times before. Tariq was beginning to tire of her and he wanted the affair to be over—with the least possible disruption to *him*.

She thought of how the situation might pan out. He might decide to stay longer in Khayarzah than he'd intended. Or he might slot in lots of extra trips abroad which would seamlessly and physically separate them. And when they finally came face to face back in the office so much time would have passed that it would be easy to consign the whole affair to history.

Easy for him, perhaps—but not for her. She hadn't done this kind of thing before. Unlike him, she was *no good at pretending.*

Wasn't it better to face the truth head-on—no matter how difficult that might be? To confront reality rather than trying to airbrush it away? Wouldn't that at least go some way to restoring her pride and making sure she didn't whittle away at her self-respect until there was nothing left but an empty husk?

She forced a smile. 'Tariq, I've been thinking.'

Something in her tone made his eyes narrow. 'Oh?'

Her heart was hammering, but she forced herself to

look directly into his eyes. 'I'm due a lot of holiday—and I was wondering if I might take the chance to use up some of my entitlement while you're away? Fiona's pretty much up to speed, and she's perfectly capable of running your office.'

Tariq stiffened as he heard the sudden formality of her tone. Holiday *entitlement*. Fiona *running his office.* He met her tawny gaze and felt a brief spear of something like pain as he realised what she was doing. Izzy was clever, he conceded. Clever enough to sense that he was cooling towards her.

'Is that really necessary?' he said.

It was a loaded question. She knew it, and he knew it too. Isobel nodded her head. 'I think so. I think we need to give each other a little space, Tariq. This...*affair* has been pretty amazing, but I suspect it's run its course—don't you?' She stared at him, willing him to say no. Longing for him to pull her into his arms and tell her she was out of her mind.

Tariq looked at her and felt a wave of admiration underpinned by a fleeting sense of regret. For, although he knew that this was the perfect solution, he was going to miss her as a lover. But relationships never stayed static. Already he could sense that she wanted more from him. More than he could ever give. And if he allowed her these weeks of absence mightn't she come back refreshed and able to put the whole thing behind her? Couldn't they go back to what they'd had before? That easy intimacy they'd shared before they had allowed sex to complicate everything?

Briefly, he acknowledged the stab of hurt pride that she should be the one to end it. But why *shouldn't* he be the one on the receiving end of closure for a change? Mightn't it do him some good?

'I think you could be right,' he said slowly.

'You do?' Could he hear the disappointment which had distorted her voice?

He nodded. 'I do. Maybe it's better we stop it now before it impacts on our working relationship.'

'Oh, absolutely,' she agreed, gritting her teeth behind her smile. Wanting to lash out at him for his naïveté. Did he really think it *hadn't* impacted on their working relationship already?

'And you deserve a break,' he said, his gaze drifting over her face. 'Why don't you get some sun on your cheeks? You look awfully pale, Izzy.'

Dimly, she registered his words, and they gave her all the confirmation she needed. He thought that a short spell in the sun was all she needed to bring her back to normal. Oh, if only it was that easy. A strange dizziness was making her head spin. For a moment she felt icy-cold beads of sweat pricking her forehead and the sudden roar of blood in her ears.

'Izzy?' He was grabbing hold of her now, hot concern blazing from his black eyes. 'For heaven's sake! What's the matter?'

His fingers were biting into her arms, but she shook them off and pulled herself away. Gripping onto the edge of the desk, she sucked in deep breaths of air and prayed she wouldn't pass out.

Tell him.

'Izzy?'

Tell him.

But the words wouldn't come—they stayed stubbornly stuck at the back of her throat and she swallowed them down again. I'll tell him when I know for sure, she thought. When he gets back.

'I'm fine, Tariq. Honestly. I just feel a little off-colour, that's all. Must have been something I ate. And now, if you'll excuse me for a minute, I'd better see about your jet. And then I'll ring through to Fiona and have her sit in on our meeting.'

She waited until she'd spoken to the airfield, and then calmed an excited Fiona's nerves, telling her that of *course* she could cope with running Tariq's office.

And it was only then that Isobel slipped along to the thankfully empty sanctuary of the bathroom, where she was violently sick.

CHAPTER ELEVEN

It was confirmed.

The blue line couldn't be denied any longer—and neither could the test Isobel had done the day before, or the day before that. Because all the tests in the world would only verify what she had known all along. And all the wishing in the world wouldn't change that fact.

She was pregnant with Prince Tariq al Hakam's baby. The man who had told her in no uncertain terms that he had no desire to have a baby was going to be a father.

Feeling caged and restless, she stared out of the window at the red bus which was lumbering down the road below. It was stuffy and hot in her tiny flat, but she felt too tired to face walking to the nearest park. She'd been feeling tired a lot recently…

Little beads of sweat ran in rivulets down her back, despite the thin cotton dress and the windows she'd opened onto the airless day. Somehow summer had arrived without her really noticing—but maybe that wasn't so surprising. In the two weeks since Tariq had flown out to Khayarzah she certainly hadn't been focussing on the weather.

Her thoughts had been full of the man whose seed was growing inside her—and she had a strange feeling of emptiness at being away from work. For once she couldn't even face going down to the cottage, where the memories of Tariq would have been just too vivid.

She'd always thought there was something slightly pathetic about people who haunted the office while they were supposed to be on holiday, and so she hadn't rung in to work either. Fiona would contact her soon enough if she needed her help, and so far she hadn't.

Which made Isobel feel even emptier than she already did. As if she had made herself out to be this fabulous, indispensable addition to the Al Hakam empire when the reality was that she could quite easily be replaced.

And she had heard nothing from Tariq. Not even an e-mail or text to tell her he was alive and well in Khayarzah. If anything proved that it was all over between them, it was the terrifying silence which had mushroomed since his departure.

There had been times when she'd been tempted to pick up the phone, telling herself that she had a perfect right to speak to him. Wasn't he still her boss, even if he was no longer her lover? But she wasn't a good enough actress for that. How could she possibly have a breezy conversation with him, as if nothing was happening, when inside her body their combined cells were multiplying at a frightening speed?

And what would she say? Would she be reduced to asking him whether it was *really* over between them—and hearing an even bigger silence echoing down the line?

No. She was going to have to tell him face to face. She knew that. And soon. But how did you break the news that he was going to be a father to a man who had expressly told you he didn't want children? And not just any father—because this wasn't just any baby. It was a *royal* baby, with *royal* blood coursing through its tiny veins—and that would have all kinds of added complications. She knew enough history to realise that the offspring of ruling families were always especially protected because royal succession was never certain. Wouldn't that make Tariq feel even more trapped into a life he had often bitterly complained about?

But that's only if he accepts responsibility for the child, taunted a voice inside her head. *He might do the modern-day equivalent of what your own father did and walk away from his son or daughter.*

Dunking a camomile teabag in a mug of boiling water, she heard the ring of her doorbell and wondered who it might be. The post, perhaps? Or some sort of delivery? Because nobody just dropped by in London on a weekday lunchtime. It could be a lonely city, she realised with a suddenly sinking heart—and this little flat was certainly no place to bring up a baby.

A baby.

The thought of what lay ahead terrified her, and she was so distracted that she'd almost forgotten about the doorbell when it rang again—more urgently this time. Her thin cotton dress was clinging to her warm thighs as she walked to the door, and she was so preoccupied that she didn't bother to check the spyhole. When she opened the door, the last person she expected to see on her step was Tariq.

She gave a jolt of genuine surprise, her tiredness evaporating as she feasted her eyes on him. She had thought of little else but him since he'd been gone, but the reality of seeing him again was a savage shock to the system. His physical presence dominated his surround-

ings just as it always did, even if the heavily hooded
ebony eyes were watchful and his mouth more unsmil-
ing than she'd ever seen it. He was wearing a shirt—
unbuttoned at the neck—with a pair of faded jeans. He
looked cool against the day, and the casual attire made
him look gloriously touchable—the irony of that did not
escape her.

'Tariq,' she said breathlessly, aware of the thunder of
her heart. 'This is a…surprise.'

He nodded. A surprise for him, too, if he was being
honest. He hadn't intended to come and see her, and yet
he'd found himself ordering his driver to bring him to
this unfamiliar part of London.

He'd spent a brutal two weeks chasing around
Khayarzah looking for his damned cousin, and the office had felt strangely empty when he had returned to
find that Izzy was still away. Not that there was anything
wrong with Fiona, her replacement. She was a sweet
girl, and very eager to please. But she wasn't Izzy. His
mouth hardened.

'Can I come in?'

'Of course you can.'

Tariq walked in and she closed the front door behind
him. It was the first time he'd ever been there, and he
walked into the sitting room and looked around. It was
a small room, and much less cluttered than her country cottage. A couple of photos stood on the bookshelf.
One was of her standing in a garden aged about eight,
squinting her eyes against the bright sunlight. One of
those images of childhood you saw everywhere. But he
had no such similar pictures of his own. There had been
no one around with a camera to record his growing up.
Apart from official ones, the only photos he had been

in were those big group ones from school—when his darkly olive complexion and powerful build had always made him stand out from the rest of his year.

He turned round as she walked into the room behind him. Her thick red curls had been scraped back and tied in a French plait, and her eyes looked huge. She looked so fragile, he thought—or was that simply because he hadn't seen her for so long?

He frowned. 'I thought you'd have been back at work by now.'

How formal he sounded, she thought. More the time-watching boss than the man who had shown her such sweet pleasure. 'You did say that I could take three weeks. And it's only been two.'

'I know exactly how long it's been, Izzy.'

They stood facing each other, as if trying to acclimatise themselves to this new and unknown stage of their relationship. It felt weird, she thought, to be alone with him and not in his arms. To have a million questions tripping off the edge of her tongue and be too afraid to ask them.

Tell him.

But the words still refused to be spoken. She told herself that she just wanted to embrace these last few moments of peace. A couple more minutes of normality when she could pretend that there was no dreaded truth to be faced. Two minutes more to feast her eyes on the face she'd grown to love and which now made her heart ache with useless longing.

'Did you find your cousin?' she questioned, raking back a strand of hair which had flopped onto her cheek.

Tariq watched as the movement drew his attention to

the lush swell of her breasts, and he felt the first twist-
ing of desire. 'Eventually,' he said.

'And was she okay?'

'I haven't come here to talk about my damned cousin,'
he said roughly.

'Oh?' Her voice lifted in hope. 'Then what *have* you
come here to talk about?'

He looked at the soft curves of her unpainted lips and
suddenly wondered just what he was fighting. Himself
or her? 'Nothing.'

'Nothing?' Her eyes were wide with confusion. 'Then
why are you here?'

'Why do you think?' he ground out, his black eyes
brilliant as temptation overpowered him and he pulled
her into his arms. 'For *this.*'

Isobel swayed as their bodies made that first contact and she felt the sudden mad pounding of her heart.
Conscience fought with desire as he drove his mouth
down on hers, and desire won hands down. Her lips
opened and she made a choking little sound of pleasure as she coiled her arms around him. Because this
was where she wanted to be more than anywhere else
in the world. Back in the arms of Tariq. Because when
she was there all her problems receded.

'Oh, *yes!*' Her helpless cry was muffled by the hard
seeking of his lips. His urgent hands were in her hair
and on her cheeks, and then skating down the sides of
her body with a kind of fevered impatience, as if he was
relearning her through touch alone. And greedily she
began to touch him back.

Tariq groaned as she began to tug at his belt. She was
like wildfire on his skin—spreading hunger wherever
her soft fingertips alighted. He could have unzipped

himself and done it to her right there. But he'd spent too many nights fantasising about this to want to take her without ceremony—and too many days on horseback not to crave the comfort of a bed.

'Where's the bedroom?' he demanded urgently.

Tell him. Before this goes any further, you have to *tell him.*

But she ignored the voice of protest in her head as she pointed a trembling finger towards a door. 'O-over there.'

Effortlessly he picked her up, as he'd done so many times before, pushing open the door with his knee and going straight over to the bed, putting her down in the centre of it. Isobel felt the mattress dip as he straddled her, one knee on either side of her body. With fingers which were not quite steady he began to unbutton her dress, and Isobel held her breath as he pulled it open. But he seemed too full of hunger to study her with his usual searing intensity, and maybe he wouldn't have noticed even if he had, for his black eyes were almost opaque with lust. Instead, he was unclipping her bra and bending his head to capture one sensitised nipple in his hungry mouth.

'I feel as if I have been in the desert,' he moaned against the puckered saltiness of her skin.

'I th-thought you had?'

'Not that kind of desert,' he said grimly.

'What kind, then?'

'*This* kind,' he clarified, his lips on her neck, his fingers hooking inside her little lace panties. 'The sexual kind. A remote place without the sweet embrace of a woman's arms or the welcome opening of her milky thighs.'

Even if they lacked emotion, the words were shockingly erotic, and Isobel lifted her head to give him more access to her neck, her fumbling fingers reaching for the buttons of his shirt and beginning to pull them open. He had come back, hadn't he? And he still wanted her. It was as simple as that. Had he found it more difficult than he'd anticipated to simply let her go?

Hope began to build in time with the growing heat of her body. She helped him wriggle out of his jeans and then the silken boxer shorts, which whispered to the ground in a decadent sigh. His shirt joined her dress on the floor and she looked up at him, strangely shy to see his powerful olive body naked on *her* bed. He seemed larger than life and more magnificent than ever—like a Technicolor character who had just wandered into a black and white film.

He moved over her, and she drew in a deep breath of anticipation. She knew his body so well, and yet she was a stranger to his thoughts. Should she tell him now? When they were physically just about as close as it was possible to be without—

'Oh!' she moaned as he entered her. Too late, she thought fleetingly, as sweet sensation shot through her body and the familiar heat began to build. Take this pleasure that you weren't expecting and give him pleasure in return. Let him see that there can still be sweetness and joy. And then maybe, maybe…

'God, you're tight,' he moaned.

'It's because you're so big,' she breathed.

'I'm always big,' came his mocking boast.

'Big*ger*, then.'

But words became redundant as he began to move

inside her, his mouth on hers as she met his every powerful thrust with the welcoming tilt of her hips.

It was the most bittersweet experience of her life. Amazing, yes—because sex with Tariq always was—but tinged with a certain poignancy, too. She was aware that things were different between them now, that nothing had been resolved. Aware too of what she still hadn't told him. And all those facts combined to heighten every one of her senses.

She felt her climax growing. The beckoning warmth which had been tantalisingly out of reach now became a blissful reality. She felt the first powerful spasm just as he gave his own ragged cry, his movements more frantic as her arms closed around his sweat-sheened back. And she was falling, dissolving, melting. Past thinking as the world fell away from her.

Minutes passed, and when she opened her eyes it was to find Tariq leaning on one elbow, his hooded eyes enigmatic as he studied her.

'Amazing,' he observed after a moment or two, a finger tracing down the side of her cheek as she sucked in a deep breath of air. 'As ever.'

'Yes.'

'You didn't ring me, Izzy.'

'I could say the same thing about you.' She looked straight into his eyes. 'Did you think I would?'

His mouth quirked into an odd kind of smile. He'd thought that her cool evaluation of their relationship having run its course had been a clever kind of bargaining tool. Had she realised that no woman had ever done that to him before? That the tantalising prospect of someone finishing with him was guaranteed to keep him interested? 'Of course I did,' he replied truthfully.

Isobel shifted restlessly. The warmth was ebbing away from her body now, and she knew she couldn't put it off much longer. Yet some instinctive air of preservation made her want to gather together all the facts first. 'Why did you come here today, Tariq?'

He smiled. 'I thought I'd just demonstrated that—to our mutual satisfaction.'

Her own smile was tight. So that had been a *demonstration,* had it? In the midst of her post-orgasmic glow, it was all too easy to forget his arrogance. 'For sex?' she queried. 'Was that why you came?'

'Yes. No. Oh, Izzy—I don't know.' He shook his head and gave a reluctant sigh, not wanting to analyse the powerful impulse which had brought him to her door today. Couldn't she just enjoy the here and now and be satisfied with that? 'Whatever it is, I've missed it.'

'If it's just sex you can get that from plenty of other women,' she pointed out.

'Then maybe it isn't just sex,' he said slowly. He lifted her chin with the tips of his fingers and she was caught in the brilliant ebony blaze of his eyes. 'Maybe what I should have said is that I've missed *you.*'

Isobel's heart missed a beat, and all the wistful longings she had suppressed as a matter of survival now came bubbling to the surface. 'You've said that before,' she whispered. 'When you've come back from a trip.'

'Yes, I know. But it was different this time—knowing that you weren't going to be here. Telling me that it was over made me realise that I could lose you—and I don't want to.'

Her heart crashed against her ribcage. 'You don't?'

'No.' He brushed his lips over hers. Back and forth and back and forth—until he could feel her shivering response. 'What we have together is better than anything I've had with anyone else. I'm not promising you for ever, Izzy, because I don't think I can do that. And I haven't changed my mind about children. But if you think you can be content with what we've got.... Well, then, let's go for it.'

His words mocked her. Taunted her. They filled her with horror at what she must now do. *Let's go for it.* That was the kind of thing a football coach said during the half-time pep talk—not a man who was telling you that you meant something really special to him. And Isobel realised what a mess she had made of everything. Despite her determination not to follow in her mother's footsteps, she had ended up doing exactly that. She had hitched her star to a man who was unavailable. In Tariq's case it wasn't because he was married but because he was emotionally unavailable. And in a roundabout way he'd just told her that he always would be.

I haven't changed my mind about children.

So now what did she do?

Feeling sick with nerves, she sat up, her unruly curls falling over her shoulders and providing some welcome cover for her aching breasts.

'Before you say any more, there's something I have to tell you, Tariq.' She sucked in a shuddering breath, more nervous than she'd ever been as he suddenly tensed. She met the narrowed question in his ebony eyes. 'You see... I'm going to have a baby.'

CHAPTER TWELVE

THE silence in the room emphasised the sounds outside, which floated through the open window. The faint roar of traffic a long way below. The occasional toot of a car. A low plane flying overhead.

Isobel stared down at Tariq's still figure, lying on the bed, and ironically she was reminded of the time when he'd lain in hospital. When he'd looked so lost and so vulnerable and her feelings for him had undergone a complete change.

But he wasn't looking vulnerable now.

Far from it. She watched the expressions which shifted across his face like shadows. Shock morphing into disbelief and then quickly settling itself into a look which she'd been expecting all along.

Anger.

Still he did not move. Only his eyes did—hard and impenetrable as two pieces of polished jet as they fixed themselves on her. 'Please tell me that this is some kind of sick joke, Izzy.'

Izzy trembled at all the negative implications behind his response. 'It's not a joke—why would I joke about something like that? I'm...I'm going to have a baby. Your baby.'

'No!' He moved then, fast as a panther, reaching down to grab his jeans before getting off the bed to roughly pull them on, knowing he couldn't face having such a conversation with her when he was completely naked. Because what if his traitorous body began to harden with desire, even as an impotent kind of rage began to spiral up inside him as he realised the full extent of her betrayal?

He zipped up his jeans and tugged on his shirt. And only then did he advance towards her with such a look of dark fury contorting his features that Isobel shrank back against the pillows.

'Tell me it isn't true,' he said, in a voice of pure venom.

'I can't. Because it is,' she whispered.

Tariq stared at her. She had known that he never wanted to be a father. She'd *known* because he'd told her! He'd even told her just now. After they'd…they'd… 'How the hell can you be pregnant when you're on the pill?'

'Because accidents sometimes happen—'

'What? You *accidentally* forgot to take it, did you?'

'No!'

'How, then?' he demanded hotly. *'How,* Izzy?'

Distractedly she held up her hands, as if she was surrendering. 'I had a mild touch of food poisoning after I ate some fish! It must have been then.'

'Must it?'

Abruptly he turned his back on her and went over to stand beside the window, staring down at the busy London street. When he turned back his face was a mask. She had never seen him look quite like that before—all cold and empty—and suddenly Isobel realised that whatever feelings he might have had for her, they had just died.

'Or was it "accidentally on purpose"?' he said slowly. 'When did it happen?'

'It was...' She swallowed. 'It was around the time when I met Zahid and Francesca.'

'You mean the *King* and *Queen*?' he corrected imperiously, unknown emotions making him retreat behind protocol—despite his conflicting feelings towards it. He remembered the way she'd held Omar that night. The way she'd looked at him over the mop of ebony curls with that soppy soft look that women sometimes assumed whenever there was a baby around.

'What? Did you look at Francesca?' he questioned. 'See another ordinary Englishwoman very much like yourself? Did you look around you and see all the wealth and status at her fingertips and think: *I wouldn't mind some of that for myself?* After all, you also had a royal lover—just as Francesca had once done. The only difference is that she didn't get herself pregnant in order to secure her future!'

If she hadn't been naked she would have lunged at him. As it was, Isobel got off the bed and grabbed at her dress to hide her vulnerability—the outward kind, anyway. For her heart was vulnerable, too—and she felt as if he had crushed it in his fist.

'I can't b-believe you could think that!' she stuttered as she started doing up the buttons, her shaking fingers making the task almost impossible.

'I suppose I can't really blame you,' he mused, almost as if she hadn't objected, a slow tide of rage still building inside him. 'Most women seem hell-bent on marriage—and the more prestigious the marriage, the better. And you can't do much better than a prince, can you?'

'You must be joking,' she hissed back. 'You might be a prince, but you also happen to be an arrogant and overbearing piece of—'

'Let's skip the insults, shall we?' he snapped, as he tried to get his head around the fact that in her belly his child grew. *His child!* A child he'd never asked for nor wanted. A child he would never be able to love...that he didn't know *how* to love. 'I thought you were into honesty, Izzy? Except now I come to think about it you haven't been very honest all the way along, have you?'

She stared at him uncomprehendingly. 'What are you talking about?'

'Just how long have you known about this pregnancy?'

She met the accusation which blazed from his face. 'For a couple of weeks,' she admitted.

A strange light entered his eyes. He looked like someone who had been trying to solve a puzzle and had just found the last missing piece stuffed down the back of the sofa. 'When we were in bed—the morning I got the phone call from Khayarzah about Leila—you knew you were pregnant then, didn't you?'

She shook her head. 'I didn't *know*. I had my suspicions, but I wasn't sure.'

'But you didn't bother to tell me? Even today you kept quiet. You let me come here and...' She'd let him lose himself in the refuge of her arms. Lulling him into sweet compliance with the erotic promise of her body.

'We had *sex*, Tariq!' she declared brutally. 'Let's not make it into something it wasn't!'

She could see the faint shock which had dilated his

eyes, but his reaction was breathing resolve into her and Isobel felt something of her old spirit return. Was she going to allow him to speak to her as if she was some worthless piece of nothing he'd found on the bottom of his shoe? As if she counted for nothing?

'I didn't tell you because I knew how you would react,' she raged. 'Because I knew that you'd be arrogant enough to think it was all some giant conspiracy theory instead of the kind of slip-up that's been happening to men and women ever since they started fornicating!'

His eyes bored into her. 'I'm assuming that marriage *is* what you want?'

Isobel's eyes widened. Hadn't he been listening to a word she'd been saying? 'You must be *mad*,' she whispered. 'Completely certifiable if you think that I'd ever want to sign up for life with a man like *you*. A man so full of ego that he thinks a woman will get herself deliberately pregnant in order to trap him.'

'You think it's never been done before?' he scorned.

'Not by me,' she defended fiercely, closing her eyes as a wave of terrible sadness washed over her. 'Now, please go, Tariq. Get out of here before either of us says anything more we might regret.'

His impulse was to resist—for he was used to calling the shots. Until he realised that this wasn't the first time Izzy had called the shots. It had been her, after all, who'd had the courage to end the relationship. And, yes, he had been arrogant enough to think that she might just be playing a very sophisticated game to bring him to heel.

But Izzy didn't do game-playing, he realised. She hadn't told him she thought she was pregnant because she'd feared his reaction—and hadn't he just proved those fears a thousand times over? He looked at the haunted expression on her whitened face and suddenly felt a savage jerk of guilt.

'I'm sorry,' he said suddenly.

Her eyes swimming with unshed tears, she looked at him. 'What? Sorry for the things you said? Or sorry that you ever got involved with me in the first place?'

He flinched as her accusations hit home. 'Sit down, Izzy.'

She ignored the placatory note in his voice. He thought he could spew out all that *stuff* and that now she'd instantly become malleable? How dared he tell her to sit down in her own home? 'I'll sit down once you've gone.'

'I'm not going anywhere until you do. Because there are things we need to discuss.'

She wanted to tell him that he had forfeited all rights to any discussion with his cruel comments. But she couldn't bring herself to do that. Because Tariq was her baby's father. And didn't she know better than anyone how great and gaping the hole could be in a child's life if it didn't have one?

'And we will,' she said, sucking in another deep breath, her hand instinctively fluttering to her still-flat belly. 'Just not now, when emotions are running so high.'

Tariq watched the unfamiliar maternal movement and something tugged at his heart. To his astonishment, he found that he wanted to ask her a million questions. He wanted to ask whether she'd eaten that day, whether she had been sleeping properly at night. He'd never asked for this baby, and he didn't particularly want it, but that didn't mean he couldn't feel empathy for the woman who carried that baby, did it?

He looked at her with a detachment he'd never used before. She *did* look different, he decided. More delicate than usual, yes—but there was a kind of strength about her, too. It radiated off her like the sunlight which caught the pale fire of her hair.

He should have been gathering her in his arms now and congratulating her. Laying a proprietorial hand over her belly and looking with pride into her shining eyes. If he had been a normal man—like other men—then he would have been able to do all those things. But he knew that all he had was a piece of ice where his heart should be, and that was why they were just gazing at each other suspiciously across a small bedroom.

But this was no time for reflection. Whatever his own feelings, this had to be all about Izzy. He had to think practically. To help her in any way that he could.

'You obviously won't be coming back to work,' he said.

Impatiently, she shook her head. 'I hadn't even thought about work.'

'Well, you don't have to. I want you to know that you don't have to worry about anything. I'll make sure you're financially secure.'

Now she observed him with a kind of fury. What? Buy her off? Did he think that she'd be satisfied with that as compensation for the lack of the marriage she'd supposedly been angling for? She thought of her own mother—how she had always gone out to work and supported herself. And hadn't Isobel been grateful for that role model? To see a woman survive and thrive and not be beaten down because her hopes of love had not materialised?

'Actually, I've decided that I want to carry on working,' she said. 'And besides, what on earth would I do all day—sit around knitting bootees? Plenty of women work right up until the final weeks. I'll…I'll look for another job, obviously.'

But she was filled with dread at the thought of going from agency to agency and having to hide her pregnancy. Who would want to take on a woman in her condition and offer her any kind of security for the future?

'You don't need to look for another job,' he said harshly. 'You could come back to work for me in an instant. Or I could arrange to have you work for one of the partners, if you don't think you could tolerate being in the same office as me.'

Isobel swallowed. She thought of starting work for someone new, with her pregnancy growing all the time. She wasn't aware of how much other people at the Al Hakam corporation knew about their affair. After all, it wasn't the most likely of partnerships, and Tariq hadn't exactly been squiring her around town. Would people put two and two together and come up with the right answer? Would her position be compromised once any new boss knew who the father of her baby was?

She stared at him, wondering what kind of foolish instinct it was which made her realise that she actually wanted to work for *him*. For there was a certain kind of security in the familiar—especially when there was so much happening in her life. At least with Tariq she wouldn't have to hide anything, or pretend. Tariq would protect her. Because, despite his angry words of earlier, she sensed that he would make sure that nothing and nobody ever harmed her, or her baby.

'I think I could just about tolerate it,' she said slowly. She met his eyes, knowing that she needed to believe in the words she was about to speak—because otherwise there could be no way forward. She had thought that if she quietly loved him then he might learn how to love her back—even if it was only a little bit. She had thought that maybe she could change him. But she had been wrong. Because you couldn't change somebody else—you could only change yourself. And Tariq didn't want love—not in any form, it seemed. He didn't want to receive it, and he didn't want to give it either. Not to her—and not to their baby.

'We must agree to give each other the personal space we need,' she continued steadily. 'The relationship is over, Tariq—we both know that. But there's no reason why we can't behave civilly towards each other.'

He was aware of an overwhelming sense of relief that she wasn't going to be launching out on her own. But something in the quiet dignity of her statement made his heart grow heavy with a gloomy realisation. As if somehow there had been something wonderful hovering on the periphery of his life.

And he had just let it go.

CHAPTER THIRTEEN

'THE press have been on the phone again, Tariq.'

Tariq looked up to see Izzy hovering in the doorway of his office, lit from behind like a Botticelli painting, with her hair falling down over her shoulders like liquid honey. Although she was wearing a loose summer dress and still very slim, at four months pregnant there was no disguising the curving softness of her belly. A whisper ran over his skin. For weeks now he had been watching her. Trying to imagine what his child must be like as it grew inside her.

And now he knew.

Aware of the sudden lump which had risen in his throat, he swallowed and raised his brows at her questioningly. 'What did they want?'

Isobel stared at the brilliant gleam of the Sheikh's black eyes, and the faint stubble on his chin which made him look like a modern-day pirate. Had she been out of her mind yesterday when she'd told him that he could accompany her to the doctor if he wanted to see her latest scan? What crazy hormonal blip had prompted *that*? She'd been expecting a curt thanks, followed by a terse refusal, but to her surprise he had leapt at the opportunity, his face wreathed in what had looked like a de-

lighted smile. A most un-Tariq kind of smile. And then
he'd acted the part of the caring father as if he actually
meant it—clucking round her as if he'd spent a lifetime
looking after pregnant women.

In fact, when he'd been helping her into the limousine—something which she'd told him was entirely unnecessary—his hand had brushed over hers, and the
feeling which had passed between them had been electric. It was the first time that they had touched since their
uneasy truce—and hadn't it started her senses screaming, taunting her with what she was missing? Their eyes
had met in a clashing gaze of suppressed desire and she
had felt an overwhelming need to be in his arms again.
A need she had quickly quashed by climbing into the
limousine and sitting as far away from him as possible.

She sighed with impatience at her inability to remain
immune to him, then turned her mind back to his question about the press. 'They were asking why the Sheikh
of Khayarzah was seen accompanying his assistant to
an obstetrician's for her scan yesterday.'

'They saw us?'

'Apparently.' Her eyes were full of appeal. 'Tariq, I
should have realised this might happen.'

Maybe she should have done. But to his surprise he
was glad she hadn't. Because mightn't that have stopped
her from giving him the chance to see the baby he had
never wanted? He still didn't know why she had done
that—and he had never expected to feel this overwhelming sense of gratitude. Perhaps he should have realised
himself that someone might notice them, but the truth
was he wouldn't have cared even if he'd known that a
million journalists were lurking around.

He hadn't cared about anything except what he was to

discover in that darkened room in Harley Street, watching while a doctor had moved a sensory pad over the jelly-covered swell of her abdomen.

Suddenly he'd seen an incomprehensible image spring to life on the screen. To Tariq, it had looked like a high-definition snowstorm—until he had seen a rapid and rhythmical beat and realised that he was looking at a beating heart. And that was when everything had changed. When he'd stopped thinking of Izzy's pregnancy as something theoretical and seen reality there, right before his eyes.

His heart had lurched as he'd stared at the form of his son—or daughter—and the doctor had said something on the lines of the two of them being a 'happy couple'. And that had been when Izzy's voice had rung out loud and clear.

'But we're not,' she had said firmly, turning to look at Tariq, her tawny eyes glittering with hurt and challenge. 'The Sheikh and I are not together, Doctor.'

Tariq had flinched beneath that condemnatory blaze—but could he blame her? Didn't he deserve comments and looks like that after his outrageous reaction when she'd told him about the baby? Even though he had been doing his damnedest to make it up to her ever since. Short of peeling grapes and bringing them into her office each morning, he was unsure of what else he could do to make it better. And he still wasn't sure if his conciliatory attitude was having any effect on her, because she had been exhibiting a stubbornness he hadn't known she possessed.

Proudly, she had refused all his offers of lifts home or time off. Had turned up her pretty little nose at his studiedly casual enquiry that she might want to join him for dinner some time. And told him that, no, she had no desire to go shopping for a cot. Or to have her groceries delivered from a chi-chi London store. Pregnant women were not invalids, she'd told him crisply—and she would manage the way she had always managed. So he had been forced to bite back his frustration as she had stubbornly shopped for food each lunchtime, bringing back bulging bags which she had lain on the floor of her office. Though he had put his foot down about her carrying them home and told her in no uncertain terms that his limousine would drop the bags off at her apartment.

Now, as she walked into his office and shut the door behind her, he realised that the Botticelli resemblance had been illusory—because beneath her pale and Titian beauty she looked tired.

'We're going to have to decide what to say when the question of paternity comes up,' she told him, wondering why it had never occurred to her that people would want to know who the father of her baby was. 'Because it will. I mean, people here have been dropping hints about it for ages, and that journalist was on the verge of asking me outright about it today—I could tell he was.'

His voice was gentle. 'What do you want to do, Izzy?'

She gave a short laugh. 'I don't think what I *want* is the kind of question you should be asking, Tariq.'

What she wanted was the impossible—to be carrying the child of someone who loved her instead of resenting her for having fallen pregnant. Someone who would hold her in the small hours of the morning when the world seemed a very big and frightening place. But those kinds of thoughts were dangerous. Even shameful. Because wasn't the truth that she still wanted Tariq to be that man—even though it was never going to happen?

To Isobel's terror, she'd discovered that you didn't just fall out of love with a man because he'd spoken to you harshly or judged you in the worst possible way.

'I don't know what I want,' she said quietly.

He stared at her, and a flare of determination coursed through him. He was aware that he could no longer sit on the sidelines and watch, like some kind of dazed ghost. Up until now he had allowed Izzy to dictate the terms of how they dealt with this because he had been racked with guilt about his own conduct. He had given her the personal space she had demanded, telling himself that it was in her best interests for him to do so. He had scrabbled deep inside himself and discovered unknown pockets of patience and fortitude. He had acted in a way which a few short months ago would have seemed unimaginable.

But it was still not enough. Not nearly enough. Close examination of her bleached face made him realise that he now had to step up to the mark and start taking control. That to some extent Izzy was weak and helpless in this situation—even though she had shown such shining courage so far.

He stood up, walked over to her, and took hold of her elbow. 'Come and sit down,' he said, guiding her firmly towards the sofa. 'Please.'

Her lips trembled and so did her body, responding instantly to his touch, and silently she raged against her traitorous hormones. But it was a sign of her weariness that she let him guide her over to the sofa.

Heavily, she slumped down and looked up at him. 'Well?'

He sat down beside her, seeing the momentary suspicion which clouded her eyes as, casting around in his mind, he struggled to find the right words to say. Clumsy sentences hovered at the edges of his lips until he realised that nobody really gave a damn about the words—only about the sentiment behind them. 'I want to tell you how sorry I am, Izzy. Truly sorry.'

She shook her head. 'You've said sorry before,' she said, blinking back the stupid tears which were springing to her eyes and which seemed never far away these days.

'That was back then—when neither of us was thinking straight. When the air was full of confusion and hurt. But it's important to me that you understand that I mean it. That in the cold light of day I wish I could take back those words I should never have said. And that I wish I could make it up to you in some way.'

She stared at him, thinking how strange it was to hear him sounding so genuinely contrite. Because Tariq didn't *do* apology. In his arrogance he thought he was always right. But he didn't look arrogant now, she realised, and something in that discovery made her want to meet him halfway.

'We both said things we shouldn't have said,' she conceded. 'Things we can't unsay which are probably best forgotten. I'm sorry that I didn't tell you about the baby sooner.'

'I don't care about that. Your reasons for that are perfectly understandable.' There was a pause. The heavy lids of his eyes almost concealed their hectic ebony glitter. 'There's only one thing I really care about, Izzy—and that's whether you can ever find it in your heart to forgive me?'

She bit her lip as hurt pride fought with an instinctive desire to make amends. Because wasn't this something she was going to have to teach her baby—that forgiveness should always follow repentance? And there was absolutely no doubt from the stricken expression on Tariq's face that his remorse was genuine.

'Yes, Tariq,' she said softly. 'I can forgive you.'

He stared at her, but her generous clemency only heightened his sense of disquiet. It made him realise then that if they wanted some kind of future together he had to go one step further.

But it wasn't easy—because everything in him rebelled against further disclosure. Wasn't it his ability to close off the painful experiences in his life which made him so single-minded? Wasn't it his reluctance to actually *feel* things which had protected him from the knocks and isolation of his childhood? Success had come easily to Tariq because he hadn't allowed himself to be influenced by emotion. To him, emotion was something that you blocked out. Because how else could he have survived if he had not done that?

Yet if he failed to find the courage to confront all the darkness he'd locked away so long ago then wouldn't he be left with this terrible lack of resolution? As if he could never really get close to Izzy again? As if he was seeing her through a thick wall of glass? And what was the point of trying to protect himself from emotional pain if he was going to experience it anyway?

'There are some things you need to know about me,' he said. 'Things which may explain the monster I have been.'

'You're no *monster*,' she breathed instantly. 'My baby's not having a monster for a father!'

'There are things you need to know,' he repeated, even though his lips curved in a brief smile at her passionate defence. 'Things about me and my life that I need to explain—to try to make you understand.'

He frowned. He struggled to put his feelings into words—because in a way wasn't he trying to make *himself* understand his own past?

'I've never had a problem with the way I live,' he said. 'My work life was a triumph and my personal life was...manageable. I was happy enough with the affairs I had. I liked women and they liked me. But as soon they started getting close—well, I wanted out. Always.'

Isobel nodded. Hadn't she witnessed it enough times before experiencing it for herself? 'And why do you think that was?' she questioned quietly.

'Because I had no idea how to relate to people. I had no idea how to do real relationships,' he answered simply. 'My mother was so ill after my birth that I was kept away from her. My father was run off his feet with the ongoing wars with Sharifah—so my relationship with him was pretty non-existent, too. And the nurses and nannies who were employed to look after me would never dare to show *love* towards a royal child, for that would be considered presumptuous. Children only know their own experience—but even if at times I felt lost or lonely I did not ever show it. In that strongly driven and very masculine environment it was always frowned on to show any weakness or vulnerability.'

Vulnerability. The word stuck to her like a piece of dry grass. It took her back to when she'd seen him lying injured on the hospital bed—for hadn't it been that selfsame vulnerability which had made her feelings towards him change and her heart start to melt? Hadn't it been in that moment when she'd started to fall in love with Tariq? When he'd shown a side of himself which he'd always kept hidden before?

'Go on,' she said softly.

'You know that they sent me away to school in England at seven? In a way, my life was just as isolated as it had been in the palace. For a while I was the only foreign pupil—and I was the only royal one. And of course I was bullied.'

'You? Bullied? Oh, come on, Tariq! As if anyone would dare try.'

He gave a wry smile. 'There are more ways to hurt someone than with your fists. I was certainly excluded on a social level—never invited to the homes of my classmates. My saving grace was that I made every sports team going and I had first pick of all the girls.' He shrugged as he realised that was about the time when he had begun to use the veneer of arrogance to protect him. 'Though of course that only increased the feelings of resentment against me.'

'I can imagine.' She sighed as she looked at him, longing to take him in her arms but too scared to dare try. Still afraid that nothing had really changed and that he would hurt her again as he had hurt her before. And besides, if he really meant it then didn't he have to come to *her*?

He saw the fear and the pain which clouded her face, and it mirrored the aching deep inside him. A terrible sense of frustration washed over him as he looked into her tawny eyes.

'Oh, Izzy—can't you see that I'm a novice at all this stuff? That for the first time in my life I don't know what to do or what to say? I've never dared love anyone before, because I didn't want to. And then when I did—I didn't know how to.'

She blinked at him, unsure whether she'd just imagined that. Love? Who'd said anything about love?

'Tariq?' she questioned, in confusion.

But he shook his head, determined to finish what he had begun, and it was like opening up the floodgates and letting his heart run free.

'In you, I found something I'd never known with any other woman. Even before we became lovers you gave me an unwitting glimpse of what life *could* be like. Those days I spent in your cottage—I'd never felt so at peace. It felt like *home*,' he realised wonderingly. 'A home I'd never really known before. Only it took me a long time to realise what was staring me in the face.' He paused. 'Just like something else which was there all the time—only I was too pig-headed to admit it. And that's the fact that I love you, Izzy. Simple as that—I just do.'

Still she didn't dare believe him—because she sensed that there would be no coming back from this. That if she discovered his words were nothing but a sham then her pain would never heal. But the light which gleamed from his ebony eyes cut through the last of her resistance. It broke through the brick wall she had erected around her heart and made it crumble away as if it were made of sand.

She lifted her fingertips to his lips.

'I love you,' he said fiercely. 'And if I have to tell you a thousand times a day for the rest of our lives before you will believe me, then so be it—I will.'

A little awkwardly, given the bump of the baby, she scrambled to her knees and sat on his lap, facing him, her hands smoothing over his face, touching his skin with a trembling delight. 'Oh, Tariq. My sweet, darling Tariq.'

'I love you, Izzy,' he said brokenly. 'And I was a stubborn fool to have tried so hard *not* to love you.' He stared at her, willing the tawny eyes to give him the only answer his heart craved. 'Just tell me it's not too late.'

'Of course it isn't,' she whispered, as she dragged in a great shuddering breath of relief. 'I think we've managed to save it in the nick of time. And thank goodness for that—because I love you too, Tariq al Hakam, and you'd better believe it. I've loved you for a long, long time, I think. Since the time you lay injured—or maybe even before that. Maybe it just took your brush with death to show me what already lay deep in my heart. And I love the baby that grows beneath my breast—*your* baby.'

He stared at her, her soft understanding suddenly hard to take. 'You are too sweet, Izzy. Too kind to a man who has done nothing but—'

'No!' she contradicted, her firm denial butting into his words. 'I'm just fighting for what is mine—and you *are* mine, Tariq al Hakam. You and this baby are all mine.'

'*Our* baby,' he said fiercely.

She touched her lips to the palm of his hand, seeing the last of the pain and regret leave his eyes as they were eclipsed by love. And she felt her heart soar as the bitterness of the past dissolved into the glorious present. 'Our baby,' she agreed.

He caught her against him and brought her head close to his. 'Beautiful, Isobel,' he whispered against her soft cheek. 'Outside and in, your loveliness shines like the moon in the night sky.'

'Poetry, too?' she questioned unsteadily. 'I didn't know you did poetry.'

'Neither did I. But then, I could never really see the point of it before.'

'Just kiss me, Tariq,' she whispered urgently. 'Kiss me quickly—before I wake up and discover this is all a dream.'

His lips grazed hers, slowly at first, and their eyes were wide open as they watched themselves kiss. And then hunger and passion and love turned the kiss into something else, and Izzy's breath began to quicken as she pressed her swollen breasts against him.

'Wait a minute,' he said, dragging his lips away and hearing her little sigh of objection. Carefully disengaging himself, Tariq got up from the sofa and went over to his desk, where he bent over and spoke into the intercom. 'Fiona, can you hold all calls, please? Izzy and I don't want to be disturbed for the rest of the day.' He turned and dazzled her with a blazing look of love. 'Do we, darling?'

In the outer office, Fiona couldn't believe it. Sheikh Tariq al Hakam had just called Isobel Mulholland *darling* and asked that they be left alone for the rest of the day! It was the sort of *unbelievable* statement which was impossible for her to keep to herself, and she went straight down to the water-cooler to tell anyone who would listen.

But perhaps that was what Tariq had intended.

Rumours were soon spreading like wildfire through the building, and by five o'clock the evening newspapers were all carrying the news that the Playboy Prince was going to be a daddy.

EPILOGUE

I<small>T WAS</small> a source of enormous frustration to Tariq that Izzy refused to marry him—no matter how many times he asked her.

'Why not?' he demanded one morning, exasperated by what he perceived as her stubbornness. 'Is it because of all those stupid accusations I made when you told me—when I said you'd deliberately got yourself pregnant in order to trap me?'

'No, darling,' she replied with serene honesty—because those days of fury and confusion were long behind them. 'That has absolutely nothing to do with it.'

'Why, then, Izzy?'

Isobel wasn't quite sure. Was it because things seemed so perfect now? So much the way she'd always longed for them to be that she was terrified of jeopardising them with unnecessary change? As if marriage would be like a superstitious person walking on a crack in the pavement—and bad luck would come raining down on them?

It had become a bit of a game—which Tariq was determined to win, because he always won in the end. But winning was not uppermost in his thoughts. Mostly he wanted to marry Izzy because he loved her—with a love which had blown him away and continued to do so.

'You'll be a princess,' he promised.

'But I don't *want* to be a princess! I'm happy just the way I am.'

'You are an infuriating woman,' he growled.

'And you just like getting your own way!'

His lips curved into a reluctant smile. 'That much is true,' he conceded.

He asked her again on the morning she gave birth to a beautiful baby daughter and he felt as if his heart would burst with pride and emotion. The nurse had just handed him the tiny bundle, and he held the swathed scrap and stared down at eyes which were blue and wide—shaped just like her mother's. But she had a shock of hair which was pure black—like his. Wonderingly, he touched her perfectly tiny little hand and it closed over his finger like a starfish—a bond made in that moment which only death would break.

His eyes were wet when he looked up and the lump in his throat made speaking difficult, but he didn't care. 'Why won't you marry me, Izzy?' he questioned softly.

Slumped back against the pillows—dazed but elated—Isobel regarded her magnificent Sheikh. This powerful man who cradled their tiny baby so gently in his arms. Why, indeed? Because she was stubborn? Or because she wanted him to know that marriage wasn't important to her? That she wasn't one of those women who were angling for the big catch, determined to get his ring on her finger? That she loved him for who he was and not for what he could give her?

'Doesn't it please you to know that I'm confident enough in your love that I don't need the fuss of a legal ceremony?' she questioned demurely.

'No,' he growled. 'It doesn't. I want to give our girl some security.'

And that was when their eyes met and she realised that he was offering her what her mother had never had. What *she* had never had. A proper hands-on father who wasn't going anywhere. Here was a man who wasn't being forced to commit but who genuinely *wanted* to. So what was stopping her?

'I don't want a big wedding,' she warned.

He bit back his smile of triumph. 'Neither do I.' But her unexpected acquiescence had filled him with even more joy than he had thought possible, and he turned his attention to the now sleeping baby in his arms. 'We'll have to think about what to call her.'

'A Khayarzah name, I think.'

'I think so, too.'

After much consultation they named her Nawal, which meant 'gift'—which was what she was—and when she was six months old they took her to Khayarzah, where their private visit turned into a triumphant tour. The people went out of their way to welcome this second son and his family into their midst—and Tariq at last accepted his royal status and realised that he had no wish to change it. For it was his daughter's heritage as well as his, he realised.

It was in Khayarzah one night, when they were lying in bed in their room in the royal palace, that Tariq voiced something which had been on his mind for some time.

'You know, we could always try to find your father,' he said slowly. 'It would be an easy thing to do. That's if you want to.'

Isobel stirred. The bright moonlight from the clear

desert sky flooded in through the unshuttered windows as she lifted her eyes to study her husband.

'What on earth makes you say that?'

Expansive and comfortable, with her warm body nestling against him, Tariq shrugged. 'I've been thinking about it ever since we had Nawal. How much of a gap there would be in my life if I didn't have her. If I had never had the opportunity to be a father.'

'But—'

'I know he deserted your mother,' he said softly. 'And I'm not saying that you have to find him. Or that even if we do you have to forgive him. I'm just saying that the possibility is there—that's all.'

It was his mention of the word *forgive* which made Isobel think carefully about his words. Because didn't forgiveness play a big part in every human life—their own included? And once her husband had planted the seed of possibility it took root and grew. Surely she owed Nawal the chance of meeting her only surviving grandparent…?

Tariq was right. It *was* easy to find a man who had just 'disappeared' twenty-five years ago—especially when you had incalculable wealth and resources at your fingertips.

Isobel didn't know what she had been expecting—but it certainly wasn't a rather sad-looking man with grey hair and tawny eyes. Recently widowed, John Franklin was overjoyed to meet her and her family. His own personal regret was that he and his wife had never been able to have children of their own.

It was a strange and not altogether comfortable moment when she shook hands for the first time with the man who had given life to her over a quarter of a century ago. But then he saw the baby, and he smiled, and Isobel's heart gave an unexpected wrench. For in it she saw something of herself—and something of her daughter, too. It was a smile which would carry on down through the generations. And there was something in that smile which wiped away all the bitterness of the past.

'You're very quiet,' observed Tariq as they drove away from John Franklin's modest house. 'No regrets?'

Isobel shook her head. What was it they said? That you regretted the things you didn't do, rather than the things you did? 'None,' she answered honestly. 'He was good with Nawal. I think they will be good for each other in the future.'

'Ah, Izzy,' said Tariq. 'You are a sweet and loving woman.'

'I can afford to be,' she said happily. 'Because I've got you.'

Their main home was to be in London, although whenever it was possible they still escaped to Izzy's tiny country cottage, where their love had first been ignited. Because maybe Francesca had been right, Tariq conceded. Maybe it *was* important that royal children knew what it was like to be ordinary.

He didn't buy the 'Blues' football team after all. It came to him in a blinding flash one night that he didn't actually *like* football. Besides, what was the point of acquiring a prestigious soccer team simply because he *could,* when its acquisition brought with it nothing but envy and unwanted press attention? He wanted to keep the cameras away from his beloved family, as much as possible. Anyway, Polo was his game.

Real men didn't prance around in a pair of shorts, kicking a ball.

Real men rode horses.

* * * * *

Mills & Boon® Hardback

January 2012

ROMANCE

The Man Who Risked It All	Michelle Reid
The Sheikh's Undoing	Sharon Kendrick
The End of her Innocence	Sara Craven
The Talk of Hollywood	Carole Mortimer
Secrets of Castillo del Arco	Trish Morey
Hajar's Hidden Legacy	Maisey Yates
Untouched by His Diamonds	Lucy Ellis
The Secret Sinclair	Cathy Williams
First Time Lucky?	Natalie Anderson
Say It With Diamonds	Lucy King
Master of the Outback	Margaret Way
The Reluctant Princess	Raye Morgan
Daring to Date the Boss	Barbara Wallace
Their Miracle Twins	Nikki Logan
Runaway Bride	Barbara Hannay
We'll Always Have Paris	Jessica Hart
Heart Surgeon, Hero...Husband?	Susan Carlisle
Doctor's Guide to Dating in the Jungle	Tina Beckett

HISTORICAL

The Mysterious Lord Marlowe	Anne Herries
Marrying the Royal Marine	Carla Kelly
A Most Unladylike Adventure	Elizabeth Beacon
Seduced by Her Highland Warrior	Michelle Willingham

MEDICAL

The Boss She Can't Resist	Lucy Clark
Dr Langley: Protector or Playboy?	Joanna Neil
Daredevil and Dr Kate	Leah Martyn
Spring Proposal in Swallowbrook	Abigail Gordon

Mills & Boon® Large Print
January 2012

ROMANCE

The Kanellis Scandal	Michelle Reid
Monarch of the Sands	Sharon Kendrick
One Night in the Orient	Robyn Donald
His Poor Little Rich Girl	Melanie Milburne
From Daredevil to Devoted Daddy	Barbara McMahon
Little Cowgirl Needs a Mum	Patricia Thayer
To Wed a Rancher	Myrna Mackenzie
The Secret Princess	Jessica Hart

HISTORICAL

Seduced by the Scoundrel	Louise Allen
Unmasking the Duke's Mistress	Margaret McPhee
To Catch a Husband...	Sarah Mallory
The Highlander's Redemption	Marguerite Kaye

MEDICAL

The Playboy of Harley Street	Anne Fraser
Doctor on the Red Carpet	Anne Fraser
Just One Last Night...	Amy Andrews
Suddenly Single Sophie	Leonie Knight
The Doctor & the Runaway Heiress	Marion Lennox
The Surgeon She Never Forgot	Melanie Milburne

Mills & Boon® Hardback
February 2012

ROMANCE

An Offer She Can't Refuse	Emma Darcy
An Indecent Proposition	Carol Marinelli
A Night of Living Dangerously	Jennie Lucas
A Devilishly Dark Deal	Maggie Cox
Marriage Behind the Façade	Lynn Raye Harris
Forbidden to His Touch	Natasha Tate
Back in the Lion's Den	Elizabeth Power
Running From the Storm	Lee Wilkinson
Innocent 'til Proven Otherwise	Amy Andrews
Dancing with Danger	Fiona Harper
The Cop, the Puppy and Me	Cara Colter
Back in the Soldier's Arms	Soraya Lane
Invitation to the Prince's Palace	Jennie Adams
Miss Prim and the Billionaire	Lucy Gordon
The Shameless Life of Ruiz Acosta	Susan Stephens
Who Wants To Marry a Millionaire?	Nicola Marsh
Sydney Harbour Hospital: Lily's Scandal	Marion Lennox
Sydney Harbour Hospital: Zoe's Baby	Alison Roberts

HISTORICAL

The Scandalous Lord Lanchester	Anne Herries
His Compromised Countess	Deborah Hale
Destitute On His Doorstep	Helen Dickson
The Dragon and the Pearl	Jeannie Lin

MEDICAL

Gina's Little Secret	Jennifer Taylor
Taming the Lone Doc's Heart	Lucy Clark
The Runaway Nurse	Dianne Drake
The Baby Who Saved Dr Cynical	Connie Cox

Mills & Boon® Large Print
February 2012

ROMANCE

The Most Coveted Prize	Penny Jordan
The Costarella Conquest	Emma Darcy
The Night that Changed Everything	Anne McAllister
Craving the Forbidden	India Grey
Her Italian Soldier	Rebecca Winters
The Lonesome Rancher	Patricia Thayer
Nikki and the Lone Wolf	Marion Lennox
Mardie and the City Surgeon	Marion Lennox

HISTORICAL

Married to a Stranger	Louise Allen
A Dark and Brooding Gentleman	Margaret McPhee
Seducing Miss Lockwood	Helen Dickson
The Highlander's Return	Marguerite Kaye

MEDICAL

The Doctor's Reason to Stay	Dianne Drake
Career Girl in the Country	Fiona Lowe
Wedding on the Baby Ward	Lucy Clark
Special Care Baby Miracle	Lucy Clark
The Tortured Rebel	Alison Roberts
Dating Dr Delicious	Laura Iding

0112 GEN STD LP

 *Mills & Boon® Online*

Discover more romance at
www.millsandboon.co.uk

 FREE online reads

 Books up to one
month before shops

 Browse our books
before you buy

...and much more!

For exclusive competitions and instant updates:

Like us on **facebook.com/romancehq**

Follow us on **twitter.com/millsandboonuk**

Join us on **community.millsandboon.co.uk**

 Visit us Online   Sign up for our FREE eNewsletter at
www.millsandboon.co.uk

WEB/M&B/RTL4/HB